Midnight's Murder:

The Hill Files, Volume 1

James Schroeder

Published by James Schroeder, 2023.

This is a work of fiction. Similarities to real people, places, or events are entirely coincidental.

MIDNIGHT'S MURDER:

First edition. November 21, 2023.

ISBN: 979-8989604012

Written by James Schroeder.

Also by James Schroeder

The Hill Files

Midnight's Murder:

Standalone

The Devil You Know

Watch for more at https://www.jamesschroederauthor.com/.

To my Niece and Nephew: Lila & Josh. I hope you continue to love reading as much as your uncle.

ACKNOWLEDGMENTS

I want to thank:

God. My Family (far too many to list at once). Hallie, Floyd, Carlos.

Those who previewed my book:

Marlene, Adam, Katie, and Brad.

My Editorial Consultants:

Nikky and Julie

All who helped me with my research:

The staff of The Berghoff, The Chicago History Museum Abakanowicz Research Center, The Des Plaines History Center, and The Chicago Police Historical Association.

A special thanks to:

Draft 2 Digital,

and

lastly, you, the reader.

CHAPTER 1

A Quiet New Year's Eve

I watched a large cloud of smoke escape my lungs, slowly pass my lips, and float up toward the ceiling of my office. I sighed heavily. After finishing the paperwork on my desk, I sat back in my chair and enjoyed the brief moment of peace. It wasn't how I planned on spending my New Year's Eve. Instead of going out on the town like the rest of humanity and finding an attractive stranger to kiss at the stroke of midnight, I had a date with my desk at the Chicago Detectives Bureau.

I've worked my fair share of late nights during my nine years on the force, so that night was nothing unusual. It was a very long night, and I was itching for any excuse to leave the office.

Having recently wrapped up a case a few weeks prior, I had no immediate cases to look into. For the most part, things were becoming relatively safe, but that didn't mean things were back to normal. Although the era of gangsters was over and

Prohibition had come to an end earlier this month, the city still had its fair share of crime and corruption.

Some of the remaining gangsters had turned from running alcohol to running drugs and even broke into the underground gambling business to mask their activities under the guise of legitimate businesses, like nightclubs, high-end restaurants, and other similar venues. There was more than enough going on to keep us boys in blue busy these days.

The famous mobster, Al Capone, had traded in his fancy suits for a pair of striped pajamas and was serving his two-and-a-half-year sentence in a federal prison in Atlanta, Georgia. He and many of his associates were answering for all their crimes. Most were serving their sentences behind bars. The only thing left for badges like me to do was find some way to keep the world from going up in flames again and do our best to get through the holiday season.

With my paperwork filled out and filed neatly in the correct folders, all that was left to do for the evening was sit in my office and wait until a new case landed in my lap, or I died of boredom—whichever came first. The last few nights had been the same. As much as I hated to admit it, tonight felt like it would be no different.

The hours ticked by without so much as a phone call. The station was mostly empty; even the chief wasn't working that night. Any police officers working were either out on patrol, booking the first boozehounds of the night, or stuck behind a desk. I wasn't too thrilled about spending the last few hours of 1933 stuck at the clubhouse, waiting for the new year to ring in without me, but I didn't have much choice.

My eyes focused on another cloud of smoke as it passed my lips. The upward swirl did little to pass the time, but the thin coils of polluted air dancing gracefully in the stillness of my office were enough to hold my attention. I was so focused on them that I almost fell out of my chair when the knock on my door disturbed the silence.

"Come in."

In walked my secretary, Dolores Anderson.

Dolores wore a tan Butterick pattern dress with four pockets and long nylon stockings that hugged her legs. Her greying hair was in the tightly curled style of a woman unwilling to accept her maturing age. Half-moon spectacles sat on the bridge of her nose, with small chains attached to the sides that kept them from falling off her head.

"Clive, there's a call for you on the other line," she said, "It sounds urgent."

"Did you catch their name?"

She shook her head. "They didn't say."

I sat up and scooted my chair closer to my desk.

"All right. Send it through," I said with a nod as she exited, "Thank you, Dolores."

When the telephone on my desk rang, I answered it immediately.

"This is Detective Clive Hill, of the Chicago Detectives Bureau. How can I help you?"

A squirrely male voice answered, his tone notably apprehensive.

"M-My name is M-Midnight ... Midnight Lawrence. I-I need to talk to someone."

"Well, Mr. Lawrence, I'm listening. What is it you need to talk about?" I replied in a calm voice.

"I-I can't say over the phone," Midnight said, his voice quivering.

"Understood. I'm in my office. If you stop by the station—"

"No!" The other man interrupted. "It's too risky. I think I'm being followed."

"Mr. Lawrence, I need you to remain calm and listen carefully. Is there somewhere nearby you can go right now—somewhere public where you can wait for me to meet you?"

"Yes," he answered, calming down slightly.

I took out a pen and paper.

"Where can I meet you?"

"I'm by a place called the Bleeding Rose." I knew the place well. It was an upscale restaurant on Chicago's south side, known for its dinner theatre and Jazz music. It was only a five-minute drive from City Hall.

"I know the place," I told him, "When you get there, ask for Joe. Tell him Hill sent you. That will get you in right away. Once you're inside, wait for me there. I'm leaving now."

CHAPTER 2

The Bleeding Rose

I arrived at the Bleeding Rose shortly after eleven o'clock. I was greeted by a giant neon sign shaped like a rose, with smaller lights below it that made it look like droplets of blood were falling from its petals. While not the most popular restaurant in the city, it still managed to pile them in around the holidays. That night was no exception.

In front of the building, a large crowd of sharply dressed people were standing on the sidewalk, waiting to gain entry for their holiday celebration. Many were none too happy when I cut to the front of the line and flashed my badge at the bouncer standing at the entrance. Several complaints were shot in my direction as I was immediately allowed inside.

Once inside, I checked my coat in with the attendant and walked to the stand near the entrance, then approached the dapper host behind it. He smiled warmly.

"Good evening. Do you have a reservation?"

I shook my head, "Not exactly. I'm Detective Hill. I'm meeting someone. 'Told them to ask for Joe."

"Ah, yes. Right this way," he said, gesturing for me to follow him.

The dining room was massive. Crowded tables surrounded an open dance floor connected to a large stage where a band was playing music for the patrons. Around the room, the waitstaff was busy taking orders, refilling drinks, and delivering trays of steaming food from the kitchen to the tables. At the same time, the occasional busboy cleared the dirty plates and returned them to the kitchen to be washed.

It wasn't the Ritz, but it was posh enough for a formal outing.

The host led me to a private table, where a very underdressed man waited nervously. The two of us stuck out like a sore thumb compared to the other guests.

The man was dressed in a navy suit jacket and a short tie. On the brim of his nose sat a pair of spectacles with lenses so thick, you'd have thought they were empty Coke bottles. He looked around the room as if he were expecting the ceiling to collapse at that moment.

"Midnight Lawrence?" I asked, taking the empty seat across from him.

"Y-Yes?" he answered; his voice had lost none of its shakiness since I'd last heard it over the telephone.

"I'm Detective Clive Hill. We spoke on the telephone a little while ago." I pulled my notebook and pencil out of my pocket. "Now, what is it you need to talk about?"

Lawrence shifted nervously. He clutched a leather attaché case as if his life depended on it. His eyes darted around the restaurant. Something, or someone, had him spooked. He was wound as tightly as a clock.

I wasn't going to get anything out of him while he was in such a frightened state.

"Are you hungry? Feel free to order whatever you like from the menu. It's on the house. I know the owner," I said, momentarily changing the subject, and quickly waved one of the waiters over. "Just a coffee for me, and whatever he wants."

After the waiter took the shaking man's order and quickly returned with a stiff drink for him, Lawrence seemed to calm down slightly—though his body was still taut.

"You've been checking over your shoulder since I sat down. Why don't you tell me what's got you so spooked, and I'll do what I can to protect you," I assured him.

Lawrence sighed, "I work—used to work—as an accountant for a man named, Cyrus Daugherty."

I knew the name well. Daugherty was a former crime boss who had his fingers in illegal drug and weapon shipments across the city for the Irish mob. As of a month ago, his deteriorating health forced him to go straight ... at least, that was what he wanted the world to think. I sensed that he hadn't left the game for good.

"I'm familiar with Mr. Daugherty's reputation," I told the worried accountant, "What led to your ... dismissal, from his employment?"

Lawrence took a long gulp of his drink. "For the past few months, I've been chiseling a little money off his profits—you know, a little here, a little there—but nothing large enough to draw attention. I didn't think he'd miss any of it," he said. "Anyway, two weeks ago, I was going to bet a sizable portion of my ... earnings at an underground casino before I was supposed to drop Mr. Daugherty's profits from last month off at the bank (I have something of a gambling problem, you see. But I've been on a hot streak lately).

"That night, I started off well—winning a bit of money at the beginning—but then, I started losing it at the Craps table. Before I knew it, I lost everything.

"The thing is, I'd placed both my money and Mr. Daugherty's in unmarked envelopes. It wasn't until I got to the bank that I realized I'd accidentally switched the envelope with Mr. Daugherty's money when I bought more chips that night. It was too late to do anything by then, so I submitted my money to my boss's account instead, hoping no one would notice that the recent deposit was smaller than it should've been.

"Everything was going fine, that is, until this morning. As soon as I knew he found out about the money, I was out of there like a hog who realized he was on his way to the butcher's block. I've been hiding ever since."

I calmly took a sip of my coffee.

"It sure looks like you've gone and cooked your own goose. I suggest you get yourself on the next train out of the city tonight. I'll drive you down to Union Station and see you off. From there, you're on your own."

Lawrence's eyes widened in fear. "I-I can't skip town tonight! I have an important meeting with someone tomorrow night that I can't miss."

My eyebrow raised in disbelief. I couldn't imagine why a man in Lawrence's position would dream of staying put when his former employer probably already had men looking all over the city for him.

Out of the corner of my eye, I spied a few unfriendly faces looking our way. Knowing better than to look at them directly, I used a small pocket mirror and pretended to pick something out of my teeth to get a better look at them.

At another table, two Irish men wearing casual tweed suits and matching newsboy hats were sitting at their table. Like us, their clothes made them easy to pick out in a crowd. Their faces were clean-shaven and covered in freckles, which stood out on their light skin. I noted a long scar on the right cheek of the man seated closest to me, likely from a knife or something similar. They seemed like the kind of goons a mobster like Daugherty would send to tail someone their boss wanted gone.

I quickly turned back to Lawrence:

"I don't think you fully understand how dire your current situation is, Mr. Lawrence," I said in a low voice.

He remained stubborn, "Detective, you don't understand, I can't miss my meeting with—"

Just then, the lights slowly began to dim. The band played fanfare as a spotlight directed everyone's attention to the stage. The Emcee took the microphone:

"It gives me great pleasure to introduce tonight's guest performance. Ladies and Gentlemen, please put your hands together for Miss Harriet Doyel!"

The crowd applauded as the red stage curtain swung open, and a beautiful lounge singer stepped out from behind it. Her pearl-colored dress shimmered in the spotlight. Expensive-looking earrings hung from her ears, and her rose-red lips popped out in contrast with her fair skin—even from a reasonable distance away, it was impossible to miss those lips. Large brunette curls hung at the sides of her head and bounced seductively with each heeled step she took.

The band began to play a slow song. When she opened her mouth and began to sing, I was mesmerized by her deep, velvety voice. I honestly couldn't have told you what song the canary was singing that night if you asked me to. I focused my attention on how her hips moved while she sang. She had the voice of a songbird with the sly moves of a feline.

She wrapped her gloved fingers around the microphone stand as her song continued. Though she stood in place, her slow, subtle movements were graceful and captivating. There was no doubt that every eye in the place was on her.

A bony man dressed in ill-fitting glad rags tossed a single rose onto the stage.

As her song ended, the canary turned and sauntered seductively behind the curtain while the audience applauded her performance. There was no denying that she deserved it.

I shook myself from my daze and turned my attention back to Lawrence, who I'd completely forgotten about during the performance. I scolded myself for getting distracted on the job. I was there to protect him, not to enjoy the show.

My gaze dropped to my wristwatch; it was eleven forty-five. We needed to get moving soon. The waiter brought a bucket of champagne on ice and placed two empty glasses on the table.

"We didn't order any champagne," I told him.

"It's complimentary. To help celebrate the new year," he said with a smile, "Would you like me to pour it now?"

I shook my head. I made it a point to never drink while I was working.

"None for us."

The waiter looked disappointed and quickly carried the bucket of chilled champagne away.

"It's almost midnight," I told Lawrence, "We should start heading over to Union to catch your train before the streets turn into a madhouse. We can't afford to miss it."

The former accountant shook his head defiantly. "I told you; I can't leave the city. I have a meeting tomorrow night."

"Well, you'll just have to reschedule it."

"I can't!"

My patience was wearing thin.

"Listen, you called me here because you're in trouble. It's my job to keep you safe. I can't do that if you won't let me get you out of the city until the heat on you dies down. If we don't get moving now, we're going to miss your train."

Lawrence thought it over for a moment.

"Fine..." he said, downing another drink in one gulp and standing up.

Judging by the way he was swaying in place slightly; it was clear he was at his limit.

"Sit back down before you fall over." I let out a sigh. The chances of us making it to the train station had dropped significantly. Like it or not, our only option was to catch the first train out of town in the morning. "You're in no condition to go anywhere. Looks like you'll have to spend the night at the station until morning."

"I'm fine," he slurred, steading himself in a less than convincing manner, "I just need to use the john before we go."

I offered to escort him to the washroom, but he swatted me away.

"I can find it on my own," he said, "I'll be back in two minutes."

A voice in my head told me not to let him go alone, but he had already headed down the hallway and turned the corner before I could say anything.

Just as I moved to follow him, the Emcee once again took the stage.

"Ladies and Gentlemen, the time is now eleven fifty-five. In a few short minutes, the new year will begin. If you all would be so kind and make your way over to the dance floor for one final dance, the countdown will begin in two minutes' time."

I looked at the table where I'd seen the shady characters earlier but quickly lost them in the crowd as all the patrons flocked to the dance floor. Trying to get through the thick sea of people was almost possible. I had no choice but to wait for Lawrence to return.

Four minutes had passed, and he had still not returned. I could wait no longer. I made my way through the crowded dance floor, held up my badge, and ordered any patrons to move aside as I slowly headed to the last place I'd seen Lawrence.

I could hear the crowd chant as the countdown began.

"Ten ... Nine ... Eight..."

I approached the door of the men's washroom and opened it.

"...Seven ... Six ... Five..."

Sprawled out on the tiled floor was Midnight Lawrence. I quickly moved to his side and searched for a pulse—but found none. By the looks of it, Lawrence had been strangled—I surmised this much by the abrasion across his neck.

The crowd continued their countdown, oblivious to the murder that had transpired:

"...Four ... Three ... Two ... One! Happy New Year!"

Fireworks exploded over the lake, filling the night sky with various colors. I looked around the washroom for Lawrence's killer and was drawn to the open window.

Wasting no time, I slipped out the window and into the alleyway. The tracks in the snow were fresh. I heard the sound of footsteps running and a car door slamming shut. I sprinted after the fleeing suspect with my standard-issue Colt Detective Special revolver drawn and rounded the corner just in time to see a black car speed away before I could get a look at the license plate. The killer had escaped.

I quickly retraced my steps and entered through the window again. Ignoring the body, I exited the washroom and discretely grabbed the attention of a passing waiter.

"Have the staff lock all the doors. Then, have the front desk call the Central Police Station. Tell them there's been a murder. No one gets in or out of this building if they aren't wearing a badge. Understand?"

The young waiter nodded his understanding.

"Do it quietly. The last thing we need is a panic," I explained, "Now, get moving."

I watched the waiter hurry toward the front entrance. I blocked the washroom door to ensure no one tampered with the crime scene. As I stood guard, I thought, *this is one hell of a way to start the new year.*

CHAPTER 3

Midnight's Murder

The boys in blue arrived promptly. It wasn't long before they had the whole building roped off. After bringing the officers on the scene up to speed on what had occurred, they spread out and began questioning the guests.

As expected, the patrons were very upset about having to spend the first hour of 1934 being questioned by the police—even more so after being told they could not leave until everyone had answered our questions. A handful of them were too intoxicated to give any credible information on what they had seen. They were given a card and told to call if they remembered anything in the morning.

Many of the guests had little to offer the investigation because they were too busy celebrating to notice anything happening around them.

After questioning most of the guests with the help of a few other officers, I had not been able to find the suspicious-looking characters I'd seen earlier that night. Before approaching anyone else, I sketched the scarred man in my notebook to help me identify him later. A short time later, most of the witnesses finished giving their statements.

"Is this everyone?" I asked a fellow detective by the name of John Foster.

He shrugged, "As far as I can tell."

"You didn't happen to see two men dressed in tweed suits and newsboy caps, by chance? One of them had a scar across his right cheek."

"Not anyone I talked to."

That's what I was afraid of.

At that moment, three more uniformed officers joined us.

"Well, we've questioned everyone," Jim Douglas said, "The staff didn't see anything while the murder was being committed. Their alibis check out."

"Any of you talk to the singer ... Miss Harriet Doyel?" I asked, "Maybe she saw something."

Mason Wayne said, "She wasn't backstage when I talked to the band."

"According to the crew backstage, Miss Doyel left right before midnight," added the rookie, Craig Lewis.

"And they saw her leave?"

"That's what they said."

The grumbling crowd was becoming more and more short-tempered with each passing minute. If we didn't start wrapping things up soon, I feared things would turn ugly.

"Clive, this crowd is starting to get restless," Wayne said, "What do you want us to do?"

I let out a sigh. "Tell them they can all go home. We've got their statements. If we need anything more, we know how to reach them."

After the order was given, the guests quickly headed toward the front entrance and out of the building, leaving us to our investigation. With no real suspects to go off of—other than the Irish weasels and a canary that flew the coop around the time of the murder—the only thing left to do was inspect the body and hope a clue turned up.

"I'd say it's high time we take a closer look at the body," I suggested, "Why don't you grab that camera of yours, Wayne, and snap a couple of photographs of the crime scene while we're at it."

Wayne nodded and quickly left to retrieve his camera from his car. He met the three of us in the men's washroom a few minutes later and began taking pictures of the crime scene to review during the investigation. I pulled out my notebook and reviewed my notes.

"This is what I know: The victim's name was Midnight Lawrence. Until recently, he worked as an accountant for Cyrus Daugherty—I'm sure you're all familiar with Daugherty's reputation.

"At around ten-twenty, I received a telephone call from the victim, who claimed he was being followed and wanted to meet me. I met him here at eleven o'clock. It became clear that he was in danger. He explained that he'd lost a large portion of Daugherty's money on the gambling table a few weeks prior.

"Daugherty found out yesterday and hired some of his button men to knock off Lawrence for losing his money.

"After hearing about the pickle he was in, I planned on getting him on the next train out of the city. At exactly eleven-fifty, the victim heads in here before we can head out, where his attacker murders him." I pointed to the open window. "After killing the victim, the suspect slipped out the window and continued down the alleyway just before I discovered the body.

"Upon noticing the open window, I followed suit and pursued the suspect on foot. Unfortunately, they gave me the clean sneak before I could read their plates. I returned inside shortly after that and had the front desk telephone the station. I'm sure you all know what happened next."

Lewis studied the scene carefully. "It looks like there was definitely a struggle. From what I can tell, the victim was taken by surprise and knocked off his feet while he was being strangled by his attacker. His larynx was fractured by whatever the killer used—likely a rope, or something similar—which caused the abrasions around the trachea. The light trauma to the back of the head suggests that the victim hit his head when he fell." He pointed out the small lump near the base of the skull.

I added the new findings to my notes and continued to listen to any other observations my colleagues had to offer. "Any other additional thoughts?"

"Well, given how loud the festivities were at the time of death, it's no wonder no one heard what was happening here," Douglas added, "If I had to guess, I'd say the killer was waiting for the victim to be alone when they approached. You mentioned earlier that the victim was being followed and that a few shady characters arrived after you met with him?"

I nodded. "There were. They also disappeared after the murder took place. One of them might've been the one I chased in the alley, but I can't say for sure. My thoughts were whoever killed Lawrence may have done so on Daugherty's orders."

"Makes sense," Foster agreed, "A man in Daugherty's position wouldn't want to get his hands dirty. Sending some of his button men after the victim gives him deniability if he was ever accused of being involved in the crime."

I muttered a muffled curse under my breath. Foster was right. There would be no way I could put the finger on Daugherty's involvement in Lawrence's murder without more solid evidence to show for it. That would not be easy. The only evidence we had that alluded to the mobster's involvement were the words of an ex-employee who'd been guilty of embezzling dough from him—but that evidence was hearsay at best. Any credible testimony that would've helped nail Daugherty sat with the rest of the unspoken secrets, rotting away on the lips of a dead man.

"Did the victim mention anything else when you talked to him?" Foster asked.

"Whenever I suggested catching the next train out of the city, he said he couldn't leave. He mentioned something about making an important meeting with someone tomorrow night."

"A meeting with who?"

"I don't know. He didn't say."

"Did he at least say where this meeting was going to take place?"

I shook my head. It looked like we were on a fast train to nowhere, with a dead end at every turn.

Just as I was considering throwing in the towel, I spotted something sticking out of one of the dead man's trouser pockets. Crouching down, I investigated further.

"What's this?"

After carefully slipping my hand into the man's pocket, I discovered a small piece of notebook paper with writing on it:

"New Year's Day. Meeting with Hal. Hal's Place. Nine PM," I read aloud.

"Is there an address on there?" Lewis asked. When I shook my head, he said what we were all thinking; "Looks like another dead end."

Without an address to wherever Lawrence and whoever this Hal-person planned on having their meeting, it was just that—another dead end. I rubbed my temples and agonized about what to do next.

Just then, Wayne perked up. "Wait a minute ... Did you say *Hal's Place*? The wife and I were there two weeks ago for our anniversary. It's a club on the other side of the city."

"Well," I admitted, "It's not much to go on, but it's a good place to start. You wouldn't happen to remember the address by chance?"

"Sure."

I scribbled the address in my notebook and the time Lawrence would meet Hal. There was nothing else the morbid crime scene could tell us. It was time to call it a night.

"Finish gathering the evidence," I instructed as I headed for the washroom door, "Make sure to pick up the attaché case I found earlier. It belonged to Midnight Lawrence. While you're at it, have Wallace take the body back to the station. We're done here."

I arrived at my apartment an hour after my shift ended at seven in the morning. I was exhausted. The night had been far more eventful than I'd expected. With a yawn, I set my badge and gun on the table in my den and leaned my weary bones against the soft cushion of the Davenport.

All in all, it was a decent-sized living space. I lived alone and rarely had company over, which I was perfectly content with. It was mostly a quiet place to rest and relax when I wasn't on shift.

A tired sigh escaped my lips. I was getting older.

Letting out another yawn, I cocked my head to the side and prepared to get some shut-eye but found my gaze drawn to the framed photograph on the side table. A sense of nostalgia filled me as I lifted it closer to my face.

The younger image of myself looked back at me. Beside him stood my former partner, Guy Duncan, and his squeeze, Lola Desiree. The photo was taken the day Guy and I officially became cops. *God, that seemed so long ago.* We had some good times together. A sea of pleasant memories came flooding back to me ... but those memories quickly began to sour.

Shaking myself from my daze, I forced myself to set it face down on the side table again. I didn't have time to reminisce about former friends and past flings I'd had over the years—I'd be there for ages from the list of dames alone—I needed rest.

I was no longer the young cop from the photograph: the stress lines and thin whisps of grey in my blond hair made that fact painfully clear. Age was beginning to catch up with me.

But there were more pressing matters at the moment. There was bound to be another late night in my future. In the meantime, I needed to keep myself sharp for the investigation. If I started slacking off on the job, I'd be no help to anyone.

With another long yawn, I rose to my feet and headed to the bedroom. Maybe I could squeeze in a few dreams about some of those past flings before I needed to get back to work at noon. I hoped so. I'd been so engrossed in the mountains of paperwork on my desk lately that I'd started dreaming about filling them out while I slept.

Whoever had killed Midnight Lawrence was still out there, and I needed to get every ounce of sleep I could fit in before the search robbed me of it completely. It was my job to find them and bring them to justice. The best place to start was to follow the one lead I had and uncover what the meeting with Hal was about.

CHAPTER 4

The Canary & The Bag of Bones

The better half of the afternoon was spent in the office of Captain William Shoemaker, the Chief of Detectives, going over my interaction with Midnight Lawrence before his murder. I spared no detail as I told him what I observed at the Bleeding Rose.

After convincing the chief that I was the perfect man suited to find Lawrence's killer, I was allowed to remain on the case. There was much more going on than either of us knew about. Come hell or high water, I would get to the bottom of it. Something inside me told me I'd find a few answers if I followed the one lead I had going for me.

That evening, I arrived at Hal's Place an hour before nine to get the lay of the land before I jumped headfirst into the lion's den.

The four-story building looked like it had been built on the ruins of an extravagant business that had gone belly up after the stock market crash in 1929—which it probably had. Most of it had been refurbished by the building's new owner—though, I found it strange that I had not been able to dig up any information on who that was when I asked around. The only name that kept turning up was the name, *Hal*. Regardless, the place was not altogether unappealing.

I entered the main lobby and traveled down it until I found a quaint little restaurant at the end of it. From there, I was directed to an empty table on the far side of the room and sat down.

Like the Bleeding Rose, there were several tables around the restaurant, with a brightly lit stage. A large crystal chandler hung from the ceiling in front of the stage. I soon discovered, upon closer examination, that it was not composed of crystal. Instead, the halfway-decent chandelier was composed of thick glass cut and polished to look like shimmering crystals. The illusion was very convincing.

I'd arrived just in time for the dinner rush. The restaurant was packed. As I looked around at the guests from the comfort of my table, I recognized a skinny man I'd seen the night before.

The man was one of the suspicious characters who'd slipped away around the time of Lawrence's murder. He had a narrow face with a wide beezer in the center of it that seemed out of place on the rest of his skeletal features. His clothes were far less formal than the ones he'd been wearing the night before. The tweed jacket he wore looked like it had been freshly pressed, and the way he fidgeted with his tie and glanced at the stage every other minute made his reason for being there clear: trying to woo a woman.

I turned my attention to a passing waiter and waved him over:

"Yes, sir? Can I get you anything?"

"An old-fashioned—Go easy on the hooch."

Under normal circumstances, I'd refrained from ordering a drink like that while working, but I made an exception that night. People tend to be able to sniff out a cop in joints like Hal's Place, especially if that cop keeps ordering drinks as virgin as a cross-legged nun. I needed to keep my cover intact.

Nodding, the waiter turned to leave, "Right away."

I grabbed his arm before he got too far.

"And a word with the owner," I added.

The waiter's smile vanished. "I'm afraid the owner has asked not to be disturbed until the performance is over." He walked away without another word before I could ask anything else. I'd also like to mention that I never received the drink I ordered that night.

At that moment, the band played a drumroll. The Emcee appeared at the side of the stage:

"Ladies and Gentlemen, put your hands together and help me welcome Miss Harriet Doyel back to the stage as she performs her next song."

The audience offered their applause as the brunette singer took the stage. It was the same canary that'd captivated me with her performance, not twenty-four hours earlier. That could not have been a coincidence.

Tonight, the beautiful dame wore a sleeveless velvet dress that made her look like a dream. Against my better judgment, I could only stare at the beautiful creature gracing the stage with her incredible voice. It was as if someone had flipped a switch off and told my mind to take five when her mouth opened. Her voice was as smooth as the velvet dress she wore.

My eyes followed her every movement when she left the stage and traveled around the room while she sang. She slowly traced the cheek of the bag of bones seated at the front table, giving him a brief moment of attention before continuing.

Eventually, she wandered over to my table and locked eyes with me. The scent of her perfume tickled my nostrils. I felt my pulse quicken at the attention. She knew her craft well.

And just like that, she moved on to the following table.

Soon, she was making the short journey back to the stage as her song ended. I noticed a stagehand whisper something to the brunette, but before I could read their lips, the bag of bones stepped in front of my view:

"What's the big idea, pal? 'You ogling my girl?" he said in an overly protective manner.

It took me a moment to process what he was saying. "Easy there, friend. I'm just passing through."

"If I had a nickel for every time I heard that..." He pointed a bony finger at me. "Consider this a warning. Next time, I might not ask so nicely. Stay away from, Miss Doyel!"

He hurried away when he noticed two stocky men approaching my table.

"You the one asking for Hal?" one of them asked.

"I am."

"Hal will see you now. Follow us."

It wasn't exactly the warm welcome I expected, but at least they asked nicely. Having no choice in the matter, I stood up and followed Hal's thugs to the elevator in the lobby and piled in.

CHAPTER 5

Hal Hath No Fury

The car took us straight to the top floor. When the doors opened, I was led to a private office.

As I entered the office, my eyes were immediately drawn to the large man seated behind the desk. Perched on the edge of it was the same canary I'd seen downstairs. I was rather impressed by how she'd managed to get up to the fourth story and into the office before anyone else in such a short time. As pretty as she was, I focused on the man behind the desk.

The man had a thick build that appeared to be more muscle than fat. He was dressed in a grey tailored suit that looked like it offered a wide range of movement. The dark-brown hair atop his head was slicked back tightly on his scalp; not one of the hairs stood on end.

He stroked the neatly trimmed lampshade mustache under his nose as he watched me approach the desk. Up close, he was more than a little intimidating.

If I were a gambling man, I'd have bet that the man in front of me was the Hal of Hal's Place.

"You must be, Hal," I said.

"Maybe," he answered, "Who's asking?"

I flashed my badge. "Detective Clive Hill, from the Detectives Bureau. I'd like to ask you a few questions."

Hal sat back in his chair, unphased by the cop in front of him.

"What seems to be the problem, detective? 'Someone complain that we swindled them during a game of *Rats and Mice*, or one of the other tables in our casino downstairs? I assure you, I run a legitimate business here."

Last time I checked, gambling was still illegal, though I was willing to overlook that offense in pursuit of getting the information I needed.

I shook my head. "That's not why I'm here. Does the name, *Midnight Lawrence,* sound familiar?"

Hal stroked his chin, "Lawrence ... Lawrence ... Can't say it rings any bells."

"It should. He was supposed to meet with you tonight at this time—At least, he was planning to, before someone murdered him last night."

Hal frowned and leaned forward in his seat. "You think I had something to do with it? Really? I ought to have you thrown out of here for even suggesting such a thing. You think you can just waltz into my place, accusing me of bumping off some Joe I ain't ever heard of—"

"I'm not accusing anyone of anything right now. I'm just following a lead. There was a note on Lawrence's body with the address and time that his meeting with you was supposed to take place. The only reason I'm here is strictly for information."

The man sat in silence, carefully weighing whether or not there was any truth to what I was saying. His eyes never looked away from me as he did so.

The dame on the edge of the desk smiled.

"All right, Gus. You've had your fun," she said, "Now, get out of my seat."

The large man did as he was told. The woman took his seat a moment later. She scooted forward and rested her slender arms on the desk.

"You'll have to forgive, Gus. He gets a little caught up in his role sometimes. My name is Harriet Doyel, but you can call me *Hal*." She turned to her bodyguards, "I'll take it from here, gentlemen. You're excused."

The guards exited, leaving the two of us alone.

Hal stood up and approached a private bar across from her desk.

"Can I offer you a drink, detective?"

I politely turned down the offer; that didn't stop her from pouring herself a glass.

"I apologize for the deception. I try to keep the fact that this place is run by a woman under wraps," she continued, taking a small sip. "You never know who'll try and take advantage of a woman in charge. Some of my competition might try and muscle their way into my position if they found out."

Her logic was sound. I'm sure plenty of men out there'd try and force her out of her business if they knew she was running things—though, something told me she was no pushover.

"I must say, I would've never pegged you as the owner," I admitted.

Hal smiled, "Then my reputation proceeds me."

"How'd a lounge singer like you come to own a place like this?"

"It's a long and dull story, I'm afraid. No reason to bore you with it." She raised an eyebrow and smiled at me through the side of her mouth, "Surely, you didn't come all this way to listen to my life story, detective. I believe you wanted to know more about Midnight Lawrence."

She was right. I couldn't let the fact that she was a woman distract me from why I was there.

"Right," I said, drawing my notebook and pencil from my pocket, "I'm sure you're aware that Midnight Lawrence was murdered just before midnight at the club you were singing at."

She nodded, "Of course. Such a shame."

"Last night, Lawrence mentioned he had a meeting with someone today that he couldn't miss. It was only after his death that I learned that he planned on meeting you here at nine o'clock this evening. Is that correct?"

"It is."

"What was the reason for the meeting?"

Hal sat back down at her desk. "Midnight Lawrence frequented my establishment since we first opened our doors. He was especially fond of the gambling area downstairs.

"A few weeks back, he lost big; over eight large. Turned out it hadn't been his money that he'd been gambling with. It belonged to his boss, Cyrus Daugherty."

"I'm aware of that much, toots," I said. "Try telling me something I don't know. What was so important about your meeting that Lawrence would risk staying here instead of catching the first train out of town? I imagine owing a mobster $8,000 would usually motivate a person to choose the latter."

The dame let out a sigh and conceded. "I never met with Lawrence in person, but he did call here yesterday morning when he realized Daugherty had gotten wise about the missing money. Naturally, I ensured Gus talked on my behalf, for appearance's sake, while I listened on the call.

"Lawrence practically begged me to give him back the money he'd lost. He said that if I didn't, he'd be a dead man. I mean, he's the one who made the mistake of gambling with his boss's money at my place, so it wasn't my problem. I'm not in the habit of just giving handouts to every bum who lost their money at my establishment. It isn't good for business.

"Still, he sounded desperate. The way he begged was almost embarrassing. I had half a mind to tell Gus to hang up the telephone and leave him to sleep in the bed he made, but what he said next piqued my interest...

"He told me he still had the books containing all of Daugherty's bank accounts, including the ones off the record, with him in his briefcase. He offered to sell them to me in exchange for the full amount he owed his boss. It sounded like he planned on somehow paying off his debt to Daugherty before he left this city for good."

That explains why he was so protective of his briefcase, I thought to myself. Unfortunately, it seemed Daugherty wanted him dead either way.

"What did you intend to do with the books when you got them?" I asked.

"Are you kidding?" Hal said, perking up, "Daugherty owns clubs all over this city. Getting my hands on those books would've helped me eliminate the competition."

I decided to change the focus of the conversation:

"You were singing at the Bleeding Rose last night, correct?" Hal nodded. "I imagine you must've had a pretty good view of the crowd from the stage. Did you happen to see any suspicious characters in the crowd?"

"Suspicious characters?" she laughed, "Honey, half my audience is suspicious characters..." She put a finger to her chin. "... But, come to think of it, I did notice a pair of fellas sitting a few tables away from the stage. They weren't part of my usual crowd."

I turned to a fresh page in my notebook and prepared to jot down her statement.

"What did they look like?"

She thought it over for a moment. "They were both wearing tweed hats with matching suits—it was dark, so I couldn't really see them well—but I could make out a pin with a black four-leaf clover on each of their collars. I think one of them might've had a scar across the side of their face..."

I quickly flipped through my notebook until I found the page with the sketch of the scarred man and showed it to her:

"Was this the man you saw last night?"

Her eyes widened, "Yes. That's him. Judging by the way they were looking around at the other tables, I could tell he and his friend weren't there for my performance."

"What about your boyfriend? I noticed he was also in the crowd last night."

Hal looked puzzled, "My boyfriend?"

"Yes. The thin bag of bones seated at the table closest to the stage. He had a single rose for you. The same man, who as it just so happens, was sitting in a similar position during your performance tonight."

Suddenly, a bulb went on in her head. "Who? Lenny Riggs? He's not my boyfriend. He just comes to all my shows. He's harmless."

I wrote the name down in my notebook.

"Don't you find that a little strange?"

She shrugged, "A beautiful girl like me, with a voice like mine, is bound to attract a couple of creeps in my line of work—Singing, that is. It comes with the territory.

"If you don't have at least one fella in the crowd who's head over heels with you once you've gone on, then you aren't really as good as you think you are."

Hal finished the drink in front of her and stood up. I could tell she was getting ready to shoo me out, so I took that as a sign I needed to wrap things up soon.

"One final question, Miss Doyel," I said, holding my pencil at the ready, "Where were you between the hours of eleven fifty-five and Midnight? A few stagehands I interviewed this morning mentioned you left the building just before the big finale. Where were you off to in such a hurry?"

"I was exhausted," the young woman admitted, "It had been a long night, so I thought it best to go home and rest. I had my driver pull my car around and take me home before I lost my voice entirely."

Judging by how she sang downstairs, I found that hard to believe.

"And the color?"

"Excuse me?'

"The color of the car that drove you home last night, what was it?" I clarified.

"White."

The car didn't match the one I'd seen fleeing the crime scene, so I didn't press the matter. I quickly finished writing her statement and prepared to leave.

"Thank you for your time, Miss Doyel. If I need anything else from you, I'll be in touch."

As soon as I reached the door, Hal stopped me:

"Detective..."

I turned to face her again. "Yes?"

"I trust you'll keep my identity a secret. I'd rather the public continue to think that the owner of this establishment is a man. I do have a reputation to uphold."

"Of course," I said with a nod before finally exiting.

As I went through the hall and boarded the elevator car, I thought about the small progress I'd made for the case. I'd recovered a few pieces of the puzzle, but hardly enough to form a clear picture with them. I needed more information.

One name kept turning up again and again during this investigation. A name that had been tossed around from the very beginning: *Cyrus Daugherty*. I figured that was a sign it was time for me to visit him.

CHAPTER 6

The Fragile Clover

At eleven o'clock, my car pulled to a large house just past the city's edge. I was immediately greeted by a tall steel gate with thick bars that prevented me from getting any closer. I was forced to park my car along the street with no alternative.

The mansion was built like a fortress. A long brick wall surrounded the perimeter of the building, making the gate the only way in or out of the place. Its upper levels towered over the high walls that protected it, with a clear view of the street—which I'm sure also doubled as perfect lookout towers. The uneasy feeling in my gut told me there was already a triggerman up top, watching my every move with a rifle pointed at my melon ... but the windows were too dark to tell for sure.

From the street, I could see a cloud of smoke rising slowly from the chimney into the cold night air. Someone was home.

The crunching sound of my boots against the snow-covered street echoed in the night as I walked toward the front gate. A husky man with a head that looked like a thick potato atop his shoulders met me on the opposite side of it with a loaded Thompson tucked under his arm.

"Whadda you want?" he asked in a gruff voice.

"I'm here to talk to your boss."

His frown deepened. "Mr. Daugherty's not taking any visitors tonight. Now, why don't you just turn around, get back in your car, and drive away."

"I'd love to. Honestly. But I need to talk to your boss tonight."

The thug gripped his gun tightly. "You soft in the head or something? I said, Mr. Daugherty is not taking any visitors. If I have to tell you again, you're going to get a bad case of lead poisoning."

I opened my overcoat and flashed my badge at him. "Threatening an officer of the law ... *Tisk, tisk* ... I'm sure your boss would love to hear about this."

The courage and confidence quickly vanished from the man's face. He quickly lowered his weapon and opened the gate.

"I didn't know you were a copper. I'm sure Mr. Daugherty would be willing to see you tonight." He gestured for me to follow him across the courtyard to the mansion's front door.

As I followed the guard, I noticed a black car resembling the one I'd seen fleeing the Bleeding Rose the night before. I mentally noted the vehicle's license plate and continued toward the door.

Once inside, the frigid temperature was replaced by an enveloping warmth. Looking around at the opulent interior, I quickly glanced at the collection of paintings framed in gold that hung on the dark emerald walls as we climbed several flights of stairs to the upper levels of the mansion. It was an impressive collection, but I didn't have time to admire them properly.

The two of us traveled through a series of hallways, passing more closed doors than I could count until we reached a pair of mahogany doors that led to what I assumed was the master bedroom. The giant thug looming there and heavy coughing in the room beyond soon confirmed my suspicion.

The larger guard wagged his head at our approach:

"Nuh-uh. Not tonight. The boss doesn't want to see no one right now."

I held my badge up to him.

"I'm sure he'll make an exception in my case."

The taller guard shot my chaperone a look of silent disapproval.

"Wait here," he said in a huff before sliding through one of the doors. He was gone no more than a minute and returned just as promptly as he'd left. "You've got ten minutes, dick. No more."

I could feel his eyes on me as I placed my hand on the doorknob opposite him and swung it open.

As I entered, I found myself in a lavish main bedroom. My eyes were immediately drawn to the king-sized bed in the center of the room. It had a large headboard and matching footboard made of dark walnut, which paired well with the dark green wallpaper that lined the surrounding walls. Under its thick green velvet sheet was a frail man in his forties—though his weakened state made him look at least ten years older. Cyrus Daugherty seemed like a shadow of the intimidating mobster he'd once been.

The lunger was dressed in a black bathrobe that covered his silk pajamas. There were more than a few streaks of silver in the crop of ginger hair atop his head, and heavy bags sagged under his tired, blue eyes; the sick man had not slept well in some time.

He let out a pained cough.

"Damn it to Hell!" he cursed in a harsh, almost hoarse voice as he beat his chest to loosen the crud in his lungs. A moment later, he caught his breath. "These damn coughs will be the death of me!"

Daugherty frowned once he caught sight of me. I'm sure if he had the energy to scowl at me he would've.

"You going to stand there staring all night, or are you going to say whatever nonsense you came here to tell me?"

I stepped closer to the bedside and drew my notebook from my pocket.

"Mr. Daugherty, my name is Detective Hill. I apologize for the late-night visit. I'm investigating a murder that happened last night just before the stroke of midnight. I have a few questions I'd like to ask you. It shouldn't take up too much of your time.

"Where were you last night between the hours of ten and midnight?"

The mobster let out a forced chuckle.

"Me? I was having a night on the town celebrating New Year's with the rest of the city." He looked at me like I was out of my gourd. "Is a dick like you really that daft? Where the hell do you think I was? 'Same place I've been for the past few months!"

I'll admit, it was probably not the best question to lead with.

"Of course, you were. How silly of me," I recovered, "Did you have any visitors last night?"

"Plenty," the sick man said, "None that a badge like you would know though."

"What about Midnight Lawrence? I'm told he was your accountant until yesterday morning. Did he pay you a visit?"

Cyrus Daugherty growled at the mention of the name.

"Lawrence? That thieving rat? Not a chance! He'll be lucky if I ever let him pay me a visit after what he did."

"What exactly did he do?" I asked, already knowing the answer.

"The bastard's been chiseling off my profits for months and using that money to feed his gambling vices!" He tried to sit up even further in frustration, but the small action exerted more energy than his fragile body would allow. Exhausted, he gave up the attempt.

"Don't get yourself excited," I said, allowing him to catch his breath, "I can tell you're frustrated. People have a nasty habit of making rash decisions in situations like yours. I hope your frustration didn't spark some kind of retaliation on your end."

Daugherty narrowed his eyes and watched me with a potent venom bubbling behind them. "What're you getting at?"

I shrugged. "Well, we have a testimony that says you ordered your men to find Mr. Lawrence once you learned he'd lost your money on the gambling table. What was the plan if they found him?"

"I don't like what you're insinuating," Daugherty warned.

"Insinuating? Never! I merely asked a simple question pertaining to what you asked your men to do in the event that they encountered Mr. Lawrence last night. Nothing more."

The mobster looked me up and down. I couldn't tell if he was sizing me up for a small aspect of the truth or a wooden box—for my sake, I hoped it was the former. He opened his mouth again:

"Sure. I sent some of my boys out to find him last night, as any businessman in my position would've done. The man stole my money, after all. As for my orders, I gave my men very specific instructions: find Lawrence and bring him back here so that he could face the proper punishment."

I stopped writing in my notebook and glanced up at Daugherty. "I'm sure you intended to use the proper *legal* avenues for said punishment."

"Of course," he answered smugly.

I decided to ease up on my questions. "How long was Mr. Lawrence in your employment?"

"Two years."

"*Two years*," I repeated, "He must have been good at his job if you kept him on for so long."

Daugherty coughed briefly before he answered. "He was decent at his job; I'll give him that. Doesn't change the fact that he was stealing from me."

"Of course not," I agreed. "Were you aware of Mr. Lawrence's gambling problem while he was employed by you?"

The mobster shrugged. "Every man's got one vice or another that strikes his fancy. It's human nature. What my men do when they're off the clock is their business. As long as it doesn't affect mine, I got no beef with them." He narrowed his eyes. "But when it does..."

He let out another heavy cough. As he raised his hand to cover his mouth, his left sleeve slid down, revealing a tattoo of a black four-leaf clover just below his wrist.

I quickly remembered that Hal had mentioned seeing pins with the same symbol on the characters watching me and Lawrence at the Bleeding Rose. It was no coincidence.

"Last night, were any of your men successful in finding Mr. Lawrence?" I asked casually.

"No. I had men watching every train, bus, and streetcar heading out of the city, as well as two men watching his place," he confessed, "A couple of my boys thought they spotted him somewhere on the South Side, but he gave them the slip before they could close in. Lost him near Thirty-First and Halsted."

That was only a few blocks from the Bleeding Rose. That couldn't have been a coincidence. I wrote down that tidbit, then asked:

"Before I forget, we received some reports of some suspicious-looking characters in that area. We were able to make a sketch of one of the men from witness descriptions we received." I handed him the rough sketch of the scarred man. "Anyone you recognize?"

Daugherty held the sketch up to the light and glanced at it. His eyebrow raised slightly. I could tell he recognized the man in the drawing.

"One of yours?" I asked.

"Once upon a time..." Daugherty admitted, handing the sketch back, "Not anymore though. 'Thought his methods drew too much attention. Bad for business if you need something done discreetly.

"What's Shifty-Shane Griffin gotten himself into this time?"

"Murder," I answered.

Daugherty let out a short laugh. "What else is new?" He coughed again; it sounded like he would hock up a lung from the effort.

To soothe his throat, he reached for a glass of water on his nightstand and drank. I waited for him to catch his breath before I continued.

"He was spotted at the scene of the crime last night. He's now a suspect in our investigation."

"Who's the unlucky stiff he offed?" the sick man asked.

"I'm surprised you don't already know. You had your men looking all over the city for him, not twenty-four hours ago."

His eyes practically lit up when he realized who I was talking about. It was hard to determine whether his surprise was genuine or artificial, but the smile on his face was genuine.

"Lawrence? You're telling me someone killed Midnight Lawrence last night?"

My silence gave him his answer.

"Shame," he continued, "I wish I could've seen it myself. Well, that takes care of that problem."

I took a step closer to his bed.

"Mr. Daugherty, it's no secret that you were the head of the Irish gang known as the Black Clovers. I know in the past you've had a very specific way of dealing with people who've double-crossed you. So, tell me the truth; did you hire someone to kill Midnight Lawrence last night?"

Of course, I didn't expect an honest answer; lying is like second nature to crooked men like Cyrus Daugherty. Even if he hadn't given the formal order to kill Midnight Lawrence, I knew he was more involved than he let on. It was no coincidence that two men from a criminal organization that he was the patriarch of just so happened to be present at the Bleeding Rose the night Lawrence was murdered.

The bedroom doors opened before I could put the screws to Daugherty more. The guard stepped in.

"Time's up, copper," he said, poking me in the back with the pistol in his hand, "You got your ten minutes. Now, it's time for you to leave."

I spied a crooked smile on Daugherty's face. It made me want to sock him right between the ears.

"Enjoy your night, detective," he said, signaling the guard to get me out.

"You've been a wonderful host, Daugherty. You truly know how to make a person feel welcome. We really must do this again sometime!" I said sarcastically before the guard shoved me through the doors and out of the bedroom.

A short time later, I reached the main hallway, escorted by the same thug who'd shown me inside, and headed toward the door. The only thing I'd learned was the identity of the goon I'd seen at the Bleeding Rose, not an address or anything else. It seemed like I was walking away empty-handed.

I noticed an open guestbook on the side table as I approached the front door. I needed to look at that book, but that wouldn't be easy with the potato-faced thug standing behind me.

Thinking quickly, I stopped just before the side table. The thug gave me a harsh shove. Using this to my advantage, I pretended to trip forward; my hands flew out to catch myself on the table, *accidentally* knocking the book and a few other items off it.

"Oh, I'm terribly sorry!" I lied as I crouched to pick up the mess on the floor. "It was an accident."

My escort quickly bent down and picked up some fallen items. While he was distracted, I quickly flipped through the guestbook until I found the page listing all the visitors that had come and gone the night before. I tore the page out and quickly slipped it into my pocket before he noticed.

"You should really be more careful shoving people around like that." I got to my feet and returned the book to tonight's page before setting it down. "There we are. Good as new."

The thug set the rest of the mess back on the table and pointed to the door. "Just get out!"

I hurried through the door and into the cold night air without further instruction. I returned to my car two minutes later and drove off.

CHAPTER 7

Key Evidence

After returning to the station, I quietly sat in my office and reviewed the new notes in my notebook for an hour or so, hoping that something would stand out. Strangely, the Irish mobster had yet to mention the missing ledgers during my talk with Daugherty. It wasn't a stretch to think that he hadn't realized they were missing yet, but a man with that much cabbage was bound to notice it sooner or later if he hadn't already.

Lawrence had intended to sell the stolen ledgers to Hal, who, in turn, intended to use said books to sabotage some of Daugherty's other clubs financially. If Daugherty knew the books were missing, he wanted to keep whatever was inside them deep under wraps.

I went to the evidence locker to look inside the leather case that Lawrence had been so protective of. If there was any truth to what Hal said about the books the accountant had planned on selling her, then there was a good chance he'd had those books on him the night he was murdered.

The leather briefcase was composed of a smooth, durable frame that protected its contents. It was impossible to tell what was inside just by looking at it. I'd need to look inside to know for sure.

As I turned the case around, my heart sank; it needed a key to open it—a key I didn't have.

I looked around the locker one last time but had no luck recovering the key for the brass locks near the handle.

"Hey, Mike," I called to the next room, "was there a key on the Lawrence body?"

The evidence supervisor poked around the corner, "What kind of key?"

"A small brass one for a briefcase lock."

"Nah. The only keys we found on him were for an Omega lock and car ignition. Nothing small enough for a briefcase. Sorry, Clive."

Then a thought struck me: what if Lawrence had intentionally left the key in his car for safekeeping before he headed into the Bleeding Rose?

"On second thought, Mike, 'mind if I take those keys off your hands for a bit?" I asked, "I'm following a hunch."

Mike walked over to me and shrugged, "I guess. Just make sure you bring them back when you're done. They're still evidence you know."

Once I had the keys, I exited with a quick hat tip.

Dawn was fast approaching when I pulled up to the Bleeding Rose. It didn't operate during morning hours, so I didn't have to worry about a crowd getting in the way of my search.

I drove around and searched the surrounding area for Lawrence's car (the only problem was I needed clarification on what it looked like). He wouldn't have parked his car at the Rose; that was just advertising his whereabouts to Daugherty's men. If I had to guess, as soon as he realized he was being followed, he'd most likely ditched his car in some alleyway before continuing on foot. The crowded streets would've been the perfect cover he needed to lose his tails.

After widening my search, I spied a parked car with a large dirty tarp draped over it in the back alleyway nine blocks from the Bleeding Rose. It seemed like the best place to hide your wheels for a while until things cooled off. If it was Lawrence's car, I knew he wouldn't have objected to my quick search.

I approached the car and removed the tarp. Underneath it was a Buckingham-Blue coupe made by Chrysler. As expected, both the driver and passenger doors were locked. I was relieved to find the keys fit perfectly in the door's Omega lock and opened with a short *click*.

Once the door was unlocked, I searched for the small brass key to Lawrence's briefcase. There was an old necktie on the car's passenger side and a folded wool blanket, but nothing else. I ducked my head by the driver's well and found it tucked under the driver's seat. Pocketing it, I continued my search for any other clues I could find. The only thing that turned up was two paper clips, a half-sucked lozenge sprinkled with dirt, and ten cents in pocket change under the seats; nothing you would call a breakthrough.

As I pushed myself back to a standing position, my hand accidentally knocked the folded blanket onto the floor. A folded sheet of paper slipped out. I lifted it from the ground and carefully unfolded it. I was surprised to find some blueprints for a new casino on it. The designs looked professional, not something scribbled hastily out of boredom.

From the looks of it, Lawrence had taken more than just Daugherty's ledgers. I had a sinking feeling the sick mobster would be more than peeved when he learned Lawrence had also taken his blueprints. I slipped the paper into my pocket and searched the car's trunk.

When I found nothing, I locked everything back up and covered the coupe with the tarp again. Though I'd hoped to find more evidence, I wasn't leaving empty-handed.

After returning to the station and signing the briefcase out from evidence again, I was allowed to take it to my office for further study. Once I'd slipped a pair of gloves over my hands, I used the brass key to unlock both of the case's locks and carefully opened it.

Inside, I found what you'd usually expect an accountant to carry around with him: a collection of sharp number-two pencils, a few extra rolls of paper for a mechanical calculator, and four accounting ledgers. A smile formed when I saw the latter items. The first two books were dated 1932, and the others covered this past year. It looked like it was all there, wrapped up nicely with a bow for Lawrence's meeting with Hal.

Though my accounting knowledge was limited, I knew enough about it to tell that those books were real. They'd need to be analyzed by more practiced eyes to get anything from them.

I poked my head out of my office when I spotted Dolores walking toward her desk to begin her shift.

"Dolores, you haven't seen Mason on your way in this morning, by chance, have you? There's a stack of ledgers on my desk from the Lawrence murder that I wanted him to take a look at."

"I'm sorry, Clive. I haven't," she said.

"Not a problem," I said with a smile, "Whenever he clocks in, would you be a dear and relay the message for me? I'll be back in the office around noon."

"Following another lead?" she asked.

"Hopefully," I answered, "I'm pulling a double shift."

"If I see him, I'll give him your message."

"Wonderful! You're the best, Dee!"

After throwing on my hat and overcoat, I pulled the folded guestbook page from my pocket and checked the list of names. Toward the bottom of the page, I found the name and address of the man I was looking for: *Shane Griffin*.

According to the guestbook, Griffin visited Daugherty on New Year's Eve at eight-fifteen that night. I suspected that the story Daugherty cooked up was a bunch of malarkey. After he left Daugherty's, that would've given him plenty of time to look for Lawrence. Either way, Griffin was at the scene of the crime at the time of the murder.

As I put my hand on the knob to leave, the telephone rang. With an annoyed sigh, I walked over to my desk and answered it.

"Hello?"

The voice on the other end of the line was sweet, flirtatious, and all too familiar.

"Good morning, detective. It's Harriet Doyel."

"Miss Doyel ... I don't remember giving you my number."

She seemed amused. "You didn't. So I figured I'd try the station and see if you were still in. Glad I caught you."

"Well, you have me. What can I help you with?"

For a person who was moonlighting as a club owner, her voice was surprisingly girlish and shy. "I ... I was wondering if you were free tonight. There were a couple of things I wanted to talk to you about alone..."

"Where'd you have in mind?

"The Walnut Grill, at seven o'clock."

I blinked. "Isn't it usually closed by then?"

"Usually," she admitted, "but being a local celebrity has its benefits. Do you think you'll be able to make it?

"Possibly ... I can't promise anything though." The thought of seeing the attractive dame was not unwelcome, but I had a busy day ahead of me at the moment. I couldn't get sidetracked. "I'll do what I can. Now, if you'll excuse me, I need to get back to work."

"I'll be waiting."

After hanging up the phone, I locked up my office and headed to get some answers from Griffin. As I turned to leave, I was approached by John Foster.

"Leaving so soon, Clive?" he asked, "Where are you off to?"

"Sorry. I can't really chat at the moment, John. I'm on my way to question a suspect involved in the Lawrence murder."

John followed me down the hall. "Gutsy move, going alone. 'You sure I can't tag along as backup?"

"Knock yourself out," I said, heading to my car. "Just try and keep up."

CHAPTER 8

Chasing Leads

John Foster and I arrived at the address Griffin had left in the guestbook, a tall fourteen-story apartment building on the city's south side that looked as dirty as sin.

After I parked the car, Foster got out and started toward the building. Before he reached the front door, I stopped him.

"You stay out here and check the perimeter," I told him, "Keep an eye on the exits, while I head in alone. If he sees two cops knocking on his door, chances are he won't talk."

Foster looked like he was about to protest but kept his mouth shut and nodded. As he started searching the perimeter, I entered the front of the building.

The main lobby was similar to the outside of the building. The wallpaper decorating the wall was damp and curling from the room's moisture. Several floorboards looked like they were rotting and wouldn't hold the weight of the feather, let alone a grown adult. A liquid (which I hoped was only water) dripped from the ceiling into a tin bucket on the floor. To say the place was rundown would be a compliment.

Casually, I walked to the front desk, where a man with a heavy five o'clock shadow sat smoking a stogie and reading the morning *Tribune*.

"Can I help you?" he asked gravelly, not looking up from his paper.

"I hope so," I said in a friendly voice, "I'm here to see, Shift—" I caught myself, "...Shane Griffin. You wouldn't happen to know which apartment he's in, would you?"

The man rolled his eyes as if asking such a simple question was a strenuous chore.

"Twelfth floor. Apartment 1219."

"Thanks," I told him, though I knew my manners were wasted on him.

I headed to the elevator and took the car to the twelfth floor. Once the doors slid open, I kept my eyes peeled for apartment 1219 as I traveled down the narrow hall. Apartment doors lined both sides of the hall. Some of them were missing numbers on their doors, but it was easy enough to tell what they were. The apartment I was looking for was on the left side, at the end of the hallway, near an additional stairwell.

I knocked on the door.

"Mr. Griffin?"

No reply.

"Mr. Griffin? I know you're in there."

I knocked again.

This time, a voice answered from the other side of it.

"Who is it? What do you want?"

"The name's Hill. I came to talk," I said, "I have a few questions I wanted to ask you. It won't take long."

"Questions? About what?"

"Questions regarding why you were at the Bleeding Rose on New Year's Eve."

There was a long pause.

"... I'll be right out," he finally said.

I heard the deadbolt and chain on the other side of the door move as the door unlocked.

Suddenly, the door swung open and the scarred man raced through it, shoving me forcefully to the ground as he sprinted toward the stairwell adjacent to his apartment.

I quickly recovered and pursued him down the steps. I'd hoped he'd cooperate and be civil, but I had a feeling that wouldn't happen. He was faster than I expected—desperate men usually are.

He skipped every few steps to put some distance between us.

"Halt!" I yelled, "I said, Halt!"

That didn't change anything. Griffin continued running down the steps like a bat out of hell. He was at least two flights ahead of me. I quickened my pace and gained ground, but he had the lead. We were one floor from ground level when he did something I hadn't expected.

Before I could reach him, Griffin climbed over the railing and dropped to the ground floor, surprisingly unharmed. He made a mad dash for the exit door while I continued after him. It looked like he was going to give me the slip.

Just as the exit door opened and Griffin made a mad break outside for freedom, Foster spotted him and chased after him.

The scarred man only made it a few feet before being tackled to the ground—both landed in a thick pile of snow.

When I finally caught up to them, Foster was already slapping handcuffs on Griffin.

"Nice work," I said, catching my breath.

"Not a problem," he said as he pulled the handcuffed man to his feet and kept a firm grip on him. "Why is it they always try and run?"

I shook my head. "I don't know, but usually the ones with nothing to hide stay put." I noticed Griffin was still struggling to get away. "Do you have him?"

The younger detective smiled. "He's not going anywhere."

A few minutes later, the two of us loaded Griffin into the backseat of the car and returned to police headquarters with our suspect in tow.

Once we returned to the station, Griffin was taken to Interrogation Room 1. I left him alone to stew a little in the hot seat until I was ready for him.

Griffin sat with his cuffed hands resting on the table and a look of defiance on his smug face. He hadn't said a word since we'd brought him in. I've been at this long enough to know when someone's playing hard to get.

A short time later, Foster and I entered the room with a file tucked under my arm.

"I apologize for the long wait, Mr. Griffin. It's been a very busy morning. Of course, this would've all gone much smoother if you hadn't run off when I showed up at your apartment this morning," I said pleasantly.

Griffin continued to stare at us with the same smug look. The two of us sat on the opposite side of the table from him.

"I'm Detective Hill. This is my colleague, Detective Foster. We have a couple of questions for you. Then, you're free to go."

Foster leaned forward. "Let's start with a simple one: Why'd you run?"

"Why do you think?" he chuckled, "A cop shows up at my door, askin' questions about where I was two nights ago.

"For someone with a reputation like mine, that means trouble! So of course, I ran. 'Doesn't take a pair of detectives to figure that out."

Foster cocked a smile, "He's not wrong."

His smile vanished when he caught sight of the look I gave him—a look that reminded him to be professional.

He let out an uncomfortable cough. "Yes ... Well ... I'm sure Detective Hill didn't mean to startle you this morning."

I ignored him and steered the conversation back on track.

"You mentioned *a reputation like yours* ... What reputation would that be exactly?"

"The kind that's smart enough to know not to answer stupid questions like that. Especially, when it's regarding places I may or may not have been."

I opened the file. "Oh, my colleague and I are well aware of your reputation, Mr. Griffin.

"It says here that you were a member of the Black Clovers. You worked as a hired killer from time to time ... Is that correct?"

The smile on Griffin's face went sour.

"We also know that you recently had a falling out with the former mobster, Cyrus Daugherty. Something about how your methods drew too much attention to his organization. Does that sound accurate?"

He rolled his eyes. "Everyone's a critic, ain't they?"

Foster cut in, "I'll wager, he was pretty pissed when you went off-book. So what happened? Did he kick you to the curb, after several sloppy jobs?"

"Mr. Griffin, while you were in Mr. Daugherty's employment, did you ever encounter a man named, Midnight Lawrence?"

Griffin raised an eyebrow at my question. "The accountant? Sure, I saw him around a couple of times—I never talked to him or anything—but he made sure my wallet was fed. So I never saw any reason to."

"And how long ago were you released from Daugherty's employment?"

The thug frowned bitterly, "Three months ago. Haven't had a job since. Daugherty made sure of that the last time I botched a job."

I jotted the information down in my notebook.

"So, you're telling me you haven't been working for Daugherty since you were let go?

"That's interesting, because the other night, you were spotted at the Bleeding Rose with another man. Witnesses say both of you were wearing a Black Clover pin on your jackets. 'Didn't think you could wear one if you weren't a member. 'Mind telling us what you were doing there?"

"Just grabbing a drink with an old pal," he answered, "or is that still illegal?"

I could tell he was lying. His answers seemed too rehearsed, as if he'd had them prepared in advance for this occasion. I kept pressing.

"So, you just happened to be there? It had nothing to do with the fact that Daugherty was looking for Midnight Lawrence that night?"

"Seems like the perfect way to get back into good graces with your old boss, if you ask me," Foster added.

The cuffed man tightened his fists until his knuckles turned white. He was starting to feel the pressure.

"Were you aware that Lawrence was at the Bleeding Rose that same night?" I asked. Before he could answer, I asked, "Is that why you paid your old boss a visit earlier that night?"

Griffin's face suddenly went pale. "H-How's you know about that?"

I continued asking my questions before he could recover.

"Did Daugherty hire you to find and murder Midnight Lawrence when you met with him at eight-fifteen? What did he want you to do?"

"Answer the question, Griffin!" Foster shouted, slamming his fist on the table. He was on his feet.

Meanwhile, Griffin's eyes widened in fear. We'd broken through the front he was putting up and exposed the truth. It scared the hell out of him.

"We were there for the singer!" he shouted.

We let his confession linger in the air for a moment. Foster calmly retook his seat.

"What did you say?"

"We were there for the singer," the defeated thug admitted; his strength was spent.

"What singer?" Foster asked.

"The dame ... Harriet Doyle..."

"You weren't there for Lawrence?"

Griffin shook his head, "No. I didn't even know he was there."

Foster and I eased back in our seats.

"What business did you want with, Miss Doyel?" I asked, my voice calm and collected.

"She's a singer at Hal's Place. The boss wanted us to grab her that night, so he could use her as leverage to strongarm her boss into selling the place to him..."

It seemed like the lounge singer's cover was still intact. If Griffin had only known the truth, I'm sure he would've been kicking himself for allowing her to slip through his fingers.

"... But she slipped away before we got backstage to nab her."

"Lucky for her," Foster said.

I focused on this new information. "Why is Daugherty so interested in Hal's Place?"

"You're tooting the wrong ringer," Griffin said, shaking his head, "I'm just the hired gun—so to speak. I don't sit in on any of the business meetings. That's Mal's gig."

"Mal?"

The scarred man nodded. "Yeah. Mal Malone. He's the one you want to talk to."

I added the name to my notebook. "Any idea where I can find him?"

"I hear he frequents the Berghoff when he's not at the boss's house," he said, giving a slight shrug, "Other than that, I couldn't tell you."

After scribbling some additional notes under the name, it became clear that the hired thug had nothing else to offer us.

I stood up and uncuffed the man.

"Thank you for your cooperation, Mr. Griffin. You're free to go. We'll have someone call you a cab, shortly."

Without another word, Foster and I exited the interrogation room.

Foster leaned in toward me once we were out of earshot. "Now I know why they call him *Shifty*. Though, I'm not sure letting a hired killer back on the streets is a good idea."

"We don't have enough evidence to prove his involvement in any of his past jobs. Besides, he gave us the information I was looking for."

"What about Malone?"

"I'm going to give Herman Berghoff a call. 'Tell him to be on the lookout for Mal Malone. If Malone is there as often as it sounds, he'll tip us off whenever Malone shows up," I said, walking toward my office, "Thanks for the assist earlier."

"Any time," he said, continuing down the hall without me.

As I turned the knob, Dolores stopped me.

"Oh, Clive. I gave your message to Mason. He has the ledgers you wanted him to look at. He said he'll let you know what he finds tomorrow."

"Thanks for the heads up," I told her, then slipped into my office.

Once at my desk, I unfolded the blueprints I'd found in Lawrence's car. I looked it over closely, taking every detail into account.

The initial design looked much grander than the layout of Hal's Place and had an air of elegance, more in line with a place like the Drake. The plans included a large restaurant with a stage for evening performances, several rooms devoted to various types of gambling, and an additional private lounge on one of the upper floors for its more privileged customers.

At the bottom corner of the plans, I noticed Daugherty's signature approving the designs. Something told me that however Lawrence had come by the plans had all been done right under Daugherty's nose.

Judging by the collection of stolen documents Lawrence had acquired, it was no surprise that the former crime boss wanted him dead. I added that note to possible motives in Daugherty's file.

After folding the blueprints and locking them in my desk drawer, I grabbed the telephone and instructed the operator to connect me with the Berghoff. Once I'd gotten through, a German man answered; his accent was thick.

"This is the Berghoff. How can I help you?"

"Herman Berghoff?" I asked.

"*Ja,* that's me," the man answered.

"Mr. Berghoff, I'm Detective Hill from the city police. I'm calling because I'm looking for a man, I'm told is a regular customer at your fine establishment. You wouldn't happen to know if a Mr. Mal Malone stopped in today, would you?"

The owner thought for a moment. "Hmm... No. I'm afraid I have not seen Herr Malone, yet. Would you like me to give him a message?"

"No that won't be necessary," I said, "I'd rather talk with him in person. If you could do me a favor and call my office the next time he drops in, that would be a big help."

Berghoff agreed, and we ended the call soon after. I casually glanced at the clock; I still had a few hours left until my shift ended. With a sigh, I lit a fresh cigarette and reviewed my notes again.

CHAPTER 9

Casual Business

I returned to my apartment sometime after five-thirty, giving me plenty of time to freshen up before meeting Miss Doyel. After showering and shaving, I changed into clean clothes I'd laid out on the bed.

Once dressed, I fastened my wristwatch and placed my revolver under my jacket before heading out for the evening.

As agreed, I met Harriet Doyel at the Walnut Grill on the seventh floor of the *Marshall Field and Company* building just before seven o'clock. The last few customers exited the restaurant as it normally closed at that time. I was surprised to see a handful of staff still around after closing up. Clearly, Harriet's status as a singer held some degree of power that allowed us to stay longer.

She was seated at a table near the towering evergreen set up in the restaurant's center, still decorated with garland and baubles from the holidays. Something about the restaurant's Circassian Walnut paneling complimented the brunette's beauty.

Harriet wore a green tray-shoulder sleeveless dress that was a shade slightly lighter than the nearby evergreen. Her face was covered in makeup powder, giving her skin a pink undertone and a light complexion, with a light touch of rose rouge on her delicate cheeks. More makeup was applied around her brown eyes, giving them a green smokey look and dark lashes that made them pop. Her lips were decorated in noir red lipstick, which only heightened her visual appeal.

She stood and smiled when she spotted me.

"Good evening, detective. I wasn't sure you were going to show."

I returned the smile despite my attempt to retain the appearance of a professional. "It looks like we have the place to ourselves. Any particular reason you wanted to meet here?"

Harriet looked up at the tree. "Not really. I just wanted to admire the tree one last time before they take it away. It's a shame they can't leave it up longer," she sighed, then gestured to the table, "Please, have a seat."

Instinctively, I walked behind her and pulled out her chair as she sat down.

"Such a gentleman."

Once seated, I moved to the chair across from her and joined her at the table.

"You clean up nicely, detective. I'd even go so far as to say you look handsome."

"I've been called worse," I said with a smile, "Although, I'm certainly enjoying the company. Why did you call me here?"

The young woman's smile widened. "I wanted to talk to you."

"Is this little social call regarding business, or pleasure?"

Harriet leaned back in her seat and crossed her shapely legs.

"Does it matter?" she asked coyly.

I shrugged. "It'll determine whether I order a coffee, or something a little stronger."

"I promise this has nothing to do with the business we discussed the last time we met."

At that moment, our server approached the table.

"Then, in that case, I'll take an old-fashioned."

"A martini for me," Harriet told the server. "Dry."

The server nodded and walked away, leaving the two of us alone.

"If you don't mind me asking, Miss Doyel—"

"Harriet," she corrected.

"*Harriet*," I repeated, "What exactly did you want to talk to me about?"

"Well, detective—"

"Clive."

Her smile widened, revealing perfectly white teeth. The drop in formal titles made the conversation feel more casual.

"Well, Clive, I've seen you a total of three times in the past two days. If we're going to be seeing each other this frequently, I think it's only fair we get to know each other a bit more."

I had to admit, the idea was appealing, but I was beginning to wonder how I'd gotten myself into this situation. Based on

Shifty-Shane Griffin's information, maybe getting to know her was a good idea.

The server returned and placed our drinks on the table, then walked away once more.

"All right," I said, "but no talking shop. I'm off duty and I'd like to enjoy this evening."

Harriet held up her martini glass. "I'll agree to that, handsome."

We *clinked* glasses and took a sip of our drinks.

"How long have you lived in Chicago?" she asked.

"I grew up in a small town outside of the city," I answered, "but I moved here as soon as I got the job at the police station. What about you?"

The brunette gave a friendly shrug. "I've always been a bit of a city girl. I just love all the lights and entertainment here. It's why I decided to become a singer."

She traced the rim of her glass with a delicate finger.

"So, is there a *Mrs. Hill* in your life?"

I nearly choked at the forwardness of her question. Usually, dames beat around the bush before asking a question like that.

"No," I said, attempting to compose myself.

"A girlfriend?"

I shook my head. "Nope."

This revelation continued to feed her interest. She uncrossed her legs and leaned in closer.

"Really? I'm surprised. I thought for sure some lucky girl had swooped down and snatched you up for herself already. How fortunate for the rest of us." She rested a hand on her chin. "A girl could go crazy around a fella like you."

I could think of a handful of women who probably had.

"I'm not the marrying type," I admitted, "I've broken too many hearts over the years to deserve the chance to settle down."

"Maybe you just haven't found the right girl." Her brown eyes met mine. "If you ask me, you're much too handsome to stay a bachelor forever."

I felt my cheeks go red. The sight made Harriet laugh.

"Oh, detective, I do believe I've made you blush," she teased. It was her turn to blush. "I'm sorry. Perhaps I'm being too forward. There's just..."

She brushed her hair behind her ear.

"...something about you that excites me. Most men who come to see my shows look at me like I'm a piece of meat. But you ... you're different.

"For the first time in a long time, I feel like a woman again."

"You are a woman," I told her.

She tilted her head and sighed. "You're something special, Clive Hill. A true gentleman."

Maybe it was the liquor or company, but I was beginning to believe her. I stared into her brown eyes and found a gentle woman longing to be seen and loved. I'd fall head over heels for her if I wasn't careful.

"I can't begin to tell you how much I've needed this," Harriet continued, "I've been so wrapped up in business lately, that I rarely get a moment to myself."

It was like she was reading a page straight out of my book.

Over the past few months, I'd developed a bad habit of throwing myself into work. I certainly had my hands busy rounding up the slowly diminishing number of gangsters polluting the streets and putting everything on hold.

"You're preaching to the choir, doll," I said, finishing my drink, "I have to say though, this is a welcome change of pace..." I flashed her a smile out of the other side of my mouth. "... And the present company isn't too shabby either."

Harriet giggled. "Do those lines usually work on all the girls you spent the night with?"

I casually leaned back in my seat. "Every now and then. The dashing good looks certainly help keep their interest."

"I'll say."

The brunette placed her hand on mine and let out a content sigh. "Oh, Clive. You are a hoot. I haven't had this much fun in ages."

"I aim to please."

I couldn't take my eyes off her. Her smile was as vibrant as the holiday trimmings around us. The twinkle in her eyes showed genuine amusement.

At that moment, I'd forgotten that she was a dame with power and influence. Tonight, though, I was not a cop, and she was not a feared club owner. We were just people. I was a man, and she was a woman. Nothing else.

Though unethical, the thought of becoming romantically involved with someone tied to the case had its appeal.

"Out of personal curiosity, if you weren't in your current occupation, what would you see yourself doing?" I asked.

Harriet hadn't expected my question but seemed more than willing to answer it.

"Who me? That's easy. I'd still be a singer. Music and entertainment have always been a deep passion of mine. It would be nice to just focus on my music for once." She smiled and returned my question. "What about you? What would you do if you weren't a cop?"

I'd never really given the idea much thought. For most of my life, I wanted to be a police officer. As a child, I enjoyed being the sheriff whenever I played Cowboys and Indians with my sister, Ivory, and all the other neighborhood kids on our block. Something about bringing order and justice to the world always interested me.

"I don't know..." I recalled that Guy Duncan used to joke about my other calling. "I've been told I have a face for working in the pictures. So, possibly something along those lines."

The brunette giggled. "I can see that. If you were, I'd pay to see all your films."

She waved the server over and handed them a large bill that more than covered the cost of our drinks.

"Keep the change."

"I can pay," I told her, feeling slightly guilty.

Harriet shook her head. "Nonsense. I invited you here. Your drink is on me."

"At least, let me walk you downstairs."

The young woman welcomed the idea. "If you insist."

She held out her hand and let me lead her to the coat room and the elevator shortly after.

Once we reached the ground floor, Harriet let out a sigh.

"I had a wonderful time tonight, Clive. You are quite the gentleman. It's a shame our careers prevent us from taking this any further. I would've liked to see where it went."

An interesting notion, indeed, I thought.

"Maybe in another life, Miss Doyel."

As the two of us walked out of the State Street side exit, the scent of smoke tickled my nose.

"Hold on," I said cautiously, "Do you smell that?"

She nodded. "Where's it coming from?"

I followed the scent around the street corner and quickly discovered a cloud of smoke rising off in the distance.

Harriet gasped at the sight. She could only speculate which building had been set ablaze.

"My club!"

I suddenly remembered what Shifty-Shane Griffin had said about Daugherty's interest in Hal's Place and wanting to use Harriet as leverage.

Apparently, the former crime boss was not as patient as I thought he was. Had he cut his losses and turned to arson to build his casino on the ashes of Hal's Place?

I pulled Harriet by the hand toward my car. "Get in! I'll drive."

I had no idea what horrible sight awaited us, but at least I could keep her safe if she tagged along.

CHAPTER 10

Up in Flames

Harriet and I arrived on the scene minutes after the Fire Department pulled up.

The whole building was engulfed in flames. Fire spilled out from all of its windows. Black smoke continued to fill the night sky. Terrified people attempted to flee the burning building, only to find the front doors locked—unfortunately, their screams were the only thing to escape its wrath.

The Fire Department went to work, trying to extinguish the tall flames. It was so bright that I had to shield my eyes with my arms as we exited my car.

Harriet ignored the brightness and ran straight toward the burning building. A nearby fireman stopped her before she got too close.

"Ma'am, we can't let you through! It's not safe! The flames are too high!"

Harriet pleaded with them repeatedly but was told to stay back and allow them to do their job. The young woman watched through tears as her world went up in flames.

I suddenly spotted the silhouette of a tall, muscular man attempting to escape through the charred doors of the front entrance with his suit jacket covering his face.

"There's a survivor!" one of the firemen called.

The tall man started running and thrust his body against the burning doors. He tried two more times before he finally broke through them. Sadly, his attempt to free the trapped civilians behind him had come too late, as the screams were suddenly silenced.

The man tumbled onto his knees and weakly crawled away from the building—part of his shirt was still on fire. Two firemen rushed over, smothered his flames, and helped him to the street. Once he let his jacket fall, I immediately recognized the man's identity. It was Gus, the man who'd pretended to be Hal the night I visited Hal's Place.

Gus was coughing and panting as he tried to expel the poisonous smoke from his lungs. His face was filthy. He looked exhausted and could barely stand upright. He wasn't standing for long.

From behind us, I heard the squeal of tires approaching. I looked back and saw a black car speeding toward us. A man standing in the passenger seat pointed to the large man.

"There he is! That's Hal! Pump him full of lead!"

I hurried over to Harriet and tackled her to the ground as the man raised his Tommy gun, pointed it at Gus, and squeezed the trigger.

A volley of bullets passed through Gus's body. The false Hal flailed violently as his vital organs were punctured during the drive-by. Several of the firefighters tried to take cover behind their trucks when the bullets started flying. Thankfully, only one or two of them were wounded in the excitement. Gus was not so fortunate.

Like a shrieking banshee, the black car sped off down the road and vanished into the night.

I quickly got off Harriet and moved to help some of the other wounded men.

The young woman hurried over to where Gus had fallen. Crimson liquid soaked onto the street from his wounds. Gus was already dead, but his employer refused to believe it.

"Gus! Get up!" she sobbed, "Please! Get up!"

At that moment, the beams supporting what remained of the burning building collapsed in a heap of smoking rubble.

Harriet looked emotionally and physically defeated by the unfortunate scene that had once been her empire. I quickly helped her up.

"We need to get you somewhere safe," I told her, "Someone wants you dead."

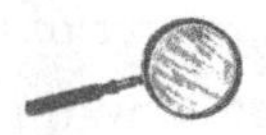

After taking her to the station and giving our statements, I offered to drive Harriet home to her apartment. As an added precaution, I volunteered to stay with her if she needed protection. Her empire was gone, and her protection was gone with it.

I locked the door and all the windows, then closed the curtains to keep our presence hidden. Making it look like she wasn't home was safer if others came looking for her.

The poor girl was shaken to the core. Gus's dried blood was still fresh on her hands. She didn't say a word after returning home. Instead, she stared blankly at nothing as if trapped in her thoughts.

Not wanting to leave the traumatized woman alone, I helped her over to the bathroom sink and gently began washing the blood off her hands. Harriet slowly started to calm down, but her hands were still trembling.

"Miss Doyel, why don't you take a shower and get yourself cleaned up? I'll be right outside the door if you need anything."

Harriet quickly grabbed my arm as I turned to leave. "N-No! Don't leave me!"

"You're safe," I assured her, "I promise. I'm not going anywhere."

"Please..." Her eyes begged me to stay, not out of selfish or lustful desire, but out of the need for human connection.

"All right..." I said, turning my back to her as she disrobed. The attractive woman slipped behind the shower curtain and turned on the water. In a matter of minutes, a cloud of steam filled the bathroom. It got so warm that I had to remove my suit jacket and unbutton the top few buttons of my shirt to keep from overheating.

Harriet's face appeared behind a crack in the curtain while the water ran, her hair wet and dripping.

"You know..." she said shyly, suppressing her grief deep down, "... You could ... join me..."

I was partially caught off guard by the invitation. I'll admit, I desperately needed a shower, but I figured I'd shower when I returned home in the morning.

"Are you sure?"

A wet hand reached through the crack and touched my arm.

Against my better judgment, I undressed and joined her in the tiny shower.

Her naked form glistened with water droplets. Most of the ash and smoke had washed out of her hair. All the makeup that had covered her face earlier had now washed down the drain, leaving her skin completely clean. Despite this, something kept the dripping woman under the running water.

"I'm ... so cold..." she said, her lips trembling.

"Do you want it warmer?" I asked.

She shook her head. There were tears in her eyes.

"No ... just ... hold me."

The young woman was probably in shock. Understandably so. She'd lost everything and watched a friend die outside her club.

I gently wrapped my arms around her and stepped under the water with her. Harriet turned and pressed her body against mine, yearning for every ounce of warmth it could provide. She rested her head on my shoulder and held me close.

For a long while, the woman in my arms wept heavily at all she'd lost as the water continued to fall on us.

The following morning was a bit better. Having rested soundly after the shower, Harriet was slowly beginning to calm down. While she slept in the comfort of her bed, I opted to take the sofa and keep watch.

The sleepy woman exited her bedroom and joined me in the living room. She was dressed in a silk robe that hugged her body in all the right ways. A yawn escaped her mouth while she stretched her arms.

"Morning," I said.

The young woman was startled momentarily but quickly remembered I was there.

"Oh, you're still here," she said, slightly confused. "Last night, did we—"

I shook my head, "No. Taking advantage of a grieving woman isn't the way I like to get a woman in bed with me."

She breathed a sigh of relief.

"After our shower, I stayed here to make sure that any unwanted visitors didn't come knocking."

A flash of embarrassment washed over the brunette's face. She was mortified.

"I ... I'm so sorry about that. I don't know what came over me."

I held up a hand to stop her. "It's quite all right. Grief has a way of making people do crazy things ... though, this was certainly a first for me."

Harriet tried to cover her reddening face with her hands. I quickly walked over to her and brushed her hands away.

"There's nothing to be embarrassed about. You've had a hard night. I was more than happy to offer you a small bit of comfort during this difficult time."

She looked up and peered into my eyes. I looked into hers and found longing and sadness but also gratitude.

"You're something else, Clive Hill," Harriet sighed in dreamlike wonder.

We held our gaze a minute longer before Harriet retreated into the kitchen.

"Can I get you something?" she called from the other room, "I could put the kettle on and make us some coffee. Are you hungry? I think I still have a couple of eggs in the cupboard."

"Coffee's fine."

She soon returned with a steaming mug of joe and sat beside me.

"Thank you," I said, taking the mug from her and lifting it to my lips.

Harriet's expression dampened as the memory of her recent loss slowly returned to the forefront of her mind.

"I can't believe it's gone..." she said distantly, placing her head in her hands, "That business was my life. What am I going to do now?"

I let out a sigh. As much as I wanted to sit there and chat with her, it was time to return to work. Right now, Harriet needed a cop, not a shoulder to cry on.

"Miss Doyel," I said, taking on a more professional tone, "Do you have any idea who might've been behind the fire last night? I'm sure you had your share of enemies. Possibly someone who really wanted you dead?"

"You want the short list, or the long one?" she said sarcastically, "Of course, I had my enemies!"

"Any who would've gone so far as to do something like this?" I decided to fill her in on what I knew. "Are you aware that Cyrus Daugherty had his sights on owning your casino?"

"Sure. He made several offers to buy the place before we opened, but I made it clear that my business wasn't for sale."

"I imagine he wasn't too thrilled with your answer," I stated. "Did he retaliate in any way, or try something to intimidate you into changing your mind?"

"Once or twice," she admitted, "but Gus scared them off before any serious damage was done."

I pulled out my notebook and collected her story. From the sound of it, Harriet thought that Daugherty had given up—clearly, that was not the case. It was time to tell her the truth.

"Under normal circumstances, I wouldn't discuss recent developments in an ongoing case with a civilian. But, given the shocking nature of what happened last night, I believe it's in your best interest to hear the truth.

"Some new information was brought to my attention regarding the two suspicious men you spotted at the Bleeding Rose on New Year's Eve.

"Originally, I believed Daugherty sent them to find and kill Midnight Lawrence for him. As it turns out, they weren't even aware that Mr. Lawrence was present that night. We have reason to believe that Daugherty hired them to kidnap you and use you to blackmail Hal into giving the casino to him in exchange for your safe return.

"Obviously they were not aware that you were the true owner. If they were, they'd have put more effort into capturing you."

Realization suddenly filled Harriet's eyes. She was beginning to understand what was going on.

"That means..." the brunette gathered, "...When those men shot Gus last night ... They were really trying to kill me."

I nodded.

"Daugherty most likely had men planted in your place last night to start the fire. 'Looks like he was tired of asking nicely. 'Probably thought it'd be easier to buy the land himself, after the previous owner's untimely demise, and build on the ashes."

"Do you think he knew that Lawrence planned on selling his ledgers to me?" she asked.

"It's hard to say for sure, but if he was looking for Lawrence's briefcase there, I doubt he would've burned the place down."

"So, Daugherty thinks I'm dead—I mean, he thinks the real owner of Hal's Place is dead," she said, correcting herself. "Does that mean I'm safe?"

Another question that I couldn't give a definite answer to. The best thing to do was to shoot straight with her.

"For the moment, but I doubt anyone is safe." I stood up and threw my coat over my shoulders. "I need to head into the office today. If I were you, I wouldn't leave this apartment today. Don't open the door for anyone. Do you understand?"

She nodded and quickly followed me to the door. "Clive, wait..."

As I turned to see what she wanted, her lips pressed against my cheek.

"Thank you ... for everything last night. Please, be safe."

I tipped my hat to her as I walked out the door.

CHAPTER 11

The Berghoff

It was half-past-eleven when I arrived at headquarters. After leaving Harriet's place, I quickly swung by my apartment and changed into some clean clothes before I headed into the office. When I got back to the station, Dolores was surprised to see me in so soon.

"Clive? What are you doing back here? I thought today was your day off?"

A day off. The idea seemed foreign to me. Even when I wasn't working, I was working. My mind was always putting the clues together—it was a gift and a curse. Cases like this required my full attention, and I wasn't about to give anything less than that.

"If only that were the case," I said pleasantly, "Is Foster in?"

Dolores nodded, "He's in his office, at the moment. Do you want me to let him know you're looking for him?"

"No. But forward any calls to his office while I'm in there."

John Foster was seated behind his desk when I entered his office. I glanced around the room. A framed newspaper article from the *Tribune* covering his first arrest hung on the wall. Pictures of his wife Evalyn and his two children (whose names escaped me) were scattered about the top of his desk. Unlike my office, John's had a more homely feel to it.

He looked up at me as I entered. "Ah, Clive. Come in. What can I do for you?"

I took a seat in the chair across from his desk.

"I was just wondering if you found anything new about the fire last night," I said, getting straight to the point.

John shook his head. "Nothing. We've had trouble identifying half the bodies we found. To put things lightly ... it's a mess."

That was putting it lightly. I didn't know what the final body count was, but given the deep stress lines on his face, I could tell the number was high.

"How's Miss Doyel?" he asked, intentionally changing the topic.

I shrugged. "She's shaken—As anyone in her position would be—but I'm sure in time, she'll be fine."

"That girl's lucky you were there last night," he added, "You saved her life."

"Any cop in my shoes would've done the same," I said modestly. "What are the chances they'll be able to rebuild the place?"

"With the owner dead, I don't see that happening for a while," he sighed. "I'm sure the bank will sell the lot once they've cleared the mess."

I wasn't about to fill him in on Harriet's big secret yet. For now, it was better to let the world believe Hal was dead.

"Do you think the Black Clovers were behind what happened last night?" John asked.

"I wouldn't put it past Daugherty. He really wanted to get his hands on that place. 'Seems like a possible motive to me."

Just then, the phone rang.

John answered it. "Hello.... Yeah... One sec..." He offered the phone to me, "It's for you."

I held the phone to my ear, "This is Hill."

"*Detektive* Hill? This is Herman Berghoff," he lowered his voice to a whisper, "The man you asked about, just walked into my restaurant."

"Thanks for the heads-up. Do what you can to keep him there. I'm heading over now." I hung up the telephone. "Excuse me. I need to chase this lead."

I headed to the door and opened it. Before I exited, I turned to John.

"While I'm out, do me a favor and have someone keep an eye on Miss Doyel's apartment. Make sure she doesn't get any unexpected visitors."

John nodded, "You seem pretty concerned with this dame's safety."

The look I gave him reminded him to mind his Ps and Qs. We were on the clock. There wasn't time to stand around and jump to conclusions—even if they were right.

He sighed, "I'll send someone over there. Though, are you sure you don't want me to come with you?"

"I'll be fine," I said, "Just get it done."

Making sure I had the final word, I headed out.

The Berghoff was flooded with customers for the lunch rush. Plenty of thirsty regulars lined up at the men's only bar, knocking back a few drinks. The place opened its doors on Adam Street in 1898 and soon became known for its famous beer and variety of German fare.

Once Prohibition went into effect, Old Man Berghoff, being the law-abiding citizen he was, focused on expanding the food services of his business and began brewing a non-alcoholic drink he called near beer. During that time, the restaurant earned a reputation for its many savory dishes. Berghoff had done pretty well for himself over the years.

When Prohibition ended earlier last month, Herman Berghoff wasted no time applying for the very first liquor license in the city, which he proudly displayed above the bar. His perseverance was justly rewarded.

As I entered through the restaurant entrance and passed the decorative stained-glass windows set in the inner walls, I admired the dark white oak architecture of the place. The numerous chandeliers that hung from the ceilings in both the bar area and the Century Room only accentuated the beauty of the wood accents and gave the place an old-world feel.

The eighty-one-year-old owner stood waiting for me near the entrance. Herman Berghoff was donning a sharp-looking striped suit that gave him the look of a respected professional. I made my way over to him.

"Is he still here?" I asked discreetly.

"Ja," Berghoff said, subtly pointing to a far table in the crowded Century Room, "Over there."

The man he was pointing to sat alone at a table with his back to us, finishing a free sandwich.

"Was he alone when he came in?" I asked.

The owner looked worried. "I-I don't think so. I didn't see anyone else with him."

A funny feeling was growing in my gut. In my experience, goons as well-connected as Malone seldom went anywhere alone. There were usually one or two other thugs nearby, ready to spring into action if things went south. The last thing I wanted was a trigger-happy gunsel making a scene that got innocent civilians caught in the crossfire.

"Wait here," I told him, "It'll be better if I go alone."

I casually walked across the checkered-tile floor and over to Malone's table.

Mal Malone had the look of a shrewd businessman. He was dressed in a dark green tweed suit with a black four-leaf clover lapel pinned to the collar of his jacket. A stripe of white ran through the otherwise vibrant ginger hair near his ears. The man was far from underfed, but he was not overweight. A glint of streetwise intelligence in his hazel eyes gave me the impression he knew how to use it to make a buck. *No wonder Daugherty had him working the business side of things.*

"You must be Mal Malone," I said.

The man looked up at me, unimpressed.

"Do I know you?" he asked, with a hint of annoyance.

"No, but I'm rather acquainted with your boss."

He lifted a brow. "Is that so? Hmmm ... I didn't think the boss liked cops much."

"Give it time," I said pleasantly, "I'm sure he'll warm up to me."

He motioned for the goons at the table behind me to stay seated. I had a feeling he didn't come in alone. The problem was that the restaurant was so crowded that there was no way of telling which table Malone's backup was sitting at.

"You got some stones on you, coming over here by yourself," Malone said, mildly impressed, "What's your interest in me?"

"I don't want any trouble. I came here to talk."

Malone crossed his arms. "Well, I'm not in the habit of talking with cops. I suggest you turn around and walk outta here before things get ugly."

His attempt to intimidate me did not phase me the slightest bit. I wasn't going anywhere. There was a gleam of overconfidence in his hazel eyes. He thought he was just as powerful as his boss, but I had one piece of dirt on him that would loosen his lips.

"Does Daugherty know you lost the blueprints for his casino?"

I'd caught him off guard with my question, even more so, considering only a handful of people knew it was missing in the first place. "How'd you know about that?"

"That's my business. Now, are you going to invite me to sit down, or do you still want me to leave?"

He'd taken the bait. His attitude changed immediately.

"Where are my manners? Please have a seat. Of course, you can join me."

I casually sat down in the chair across from him. As an added precaution, I unbuttoned my overcoat and suit jacket for quick access to my revolver if the need for it arose.

A moment later, the waiter approached the table. He wore a black jacket over a white formal apron that stopped at his shins, with a black bow tie that completed the look. Besides being known for its food and drinks, the Berghoff prided itself on its very professional service, so much so that its waiters remembered everyone's orders without needing to write them down.

The waiter carried a tray with a glass of Dortmunder-style beer and set it on the table before Malone. "Here you are, sir."

Malone drew a shiny nickel from his trouser pockets and flipped it over to the waiter with his thumb. The waiter caught the payment and placed it in his jacket pocket with his free hand.

"Thank you," he said politely before turning to me, "Anything for you, sir?"

Under normal circumstances, I would've ordered a breaded veal cutlet topped with savory brown mushroom sauce and a side of red cabbage—but I wasn't there to eat.

"Nothing for me," I politely replied in turn.

The waiter nodded and retreated to the kitchen.

Malone took a sip of his beer. "You said you came here to talk, so let's talk. Make it quick, though, I got things to do today."

"So I've heard. 'Word on the street is you've been running Daugherty's business for him since he got sick. From the look of things, I'd say that puts you pretty high up on the list of candidates likely to inherit everything once your boss bites the big one."

The businessman smiled at the notion. "I'm not complaining. 'Plenty of money in this line of work."

"Sounds like it." I diverted the conversation away from buttering up his ego, "Speaking of money, did you work closely with Midnight Lawrence?"

He shrugged. "Every now and then. He handled the finances, while I kept all the cogs turning for Mr. Daugherty. We didn't exactly see much of each other on a day-to-day basis. 'Heard he turned up dead a few nights ago—can't say I'm surprised. The man practically lived at the casinos in this city."

"So you were aware of his gambling habits, then?" I surmised.

"Everyone was," Malone chuckled, "He was even banned from gambling in the boss's casinos, once he started working for him."

"Because he was losing more money than he could pay back?"

"No. He was *winning* more money than the boss cared to part with. He nearly cleaned out one of the boss's casinos playing cards one night. In exchange for his life, he offered to work for Mr. Daugherty as his accountant."

Interesting. So, it was Lawrence's gambling habits that got him involved with Daugherty. No wonder Lawrence was chiseling money from him. As much as I wanted to write all the new information down in my notebook, keeping my full attention on Malone and the men behind me was more important. If I lowered my guard for even an instant, I might find myself in a new pot of boiling water that I couldn't get out of. I wasn't about to take that risk. Still, I needed to keep him talking.

"Speaking of casinos, I'm told your boss tried to buy Hal's Place before it opened."

Malone let out a loud laugh.

"He sure did. More than once too. 'Offered the owner double what the place was worth, but the bastard refused to sell."

"Why'd he want that building so badly? He owns a number of clubs around here already," I asked, "What was the draw to that particular location?"

The man leaned back. "Mr. Daugherty has an eye for prime real estate. That building was sure to bring in plenty of business, being so close to the heart of the city. He had his eye on that spot long before Hal outbid him for it."

I made a mental note for later.

"I imagine you've heard that Hal's Place burned down last night. Lots of people died in the fire."

Malone lifted his drink and shrugged. The man showed no concern in the slightest—even fake concern would have been a more appropriate response to the situation—but he showed none.

"Accidents happen," he said impartially, "Maybe the building wasn't as safe as Hal thought it was. I guarantee something like that wouldn't have happened if Mr. Daugherty owned the place." He took another swig of his beer.

"It was no accident," my voice took on a serious tone, "A car arrived shortly after the fire started to finish off any survivors. They gunned down Hal and wounded a handful of firemen on the scene before they sped off."

Malone shook his head, "Hmmm... Just when you think it's safe to go out again, something like this happens. These are crazy times we live in." He suddenly raised an eyebrow, like a devil hatching a nefarious idea. "With the owner dead, that means that lot will be up for grabs then, won't it?"

"And I suppose your boss will be the first in line to buy it?"

"He's never been one to turn down a business opportunity when it presents itself," the businessman admitted nonchalantly.

"That might take a while, considering Lawrence ran off with Daugherty's account books and casino blueprints the night he was murdered," I pointed out.

Malone's eyes narrowed. "He's the yuck who stole from Mr. Daugherty?"

"Happened right under his nose."

"That's unfortunate." The thug in glad rags stroked his chin. "Do you have any idea where Lawrence stashed them?"

"Of course, I do," I said plainly. "I know exactly where they are. But I can't discuss the details of an ongoing investigation."

I looked over my shoulder and noticed the thugs behind me stir.

"What? Are you going to have your pals over there, muscle me into telling you where the plans are?"

"No..." I heard the *click* of a pistol's hammer from under the table. "... I'm going to ask you myself. If I was you, I'd hand over those blueprints right now and tell me where Lawrence hid Mr. Daugherty's books."

I remained calm, "I'm afraid I can't do that. I don't have them on me right now. You didn't think I'd be foolish enough to bring them here with me, did you?"

Malone considered this information. A moment later, I heard him switch the safety back on.

"I suppose you're not as dumb as you look," he said, tucking the pistol back in his jacket. He then drew his wallet and flipped through the bills inside. "All right then. I see what's going on here. Name your price?"

Was this Joker trying to bribe me into giving up evidence? I shook my head disapprovingly.

"They're not for sale, and neither am I. Your boss was behind what happened at Hal's Place last night. He can deny it all he wants, but I know the truth.

"You can tell Daugherty that I'm not going to stand by and let him go around this city murdering innocent civilians so he can expand on an empire he's not even going to be around to see. One way or another, he's going to answer for his crimes."

"Is that so?" Malone asked sarcastically, "What crimes are you referring to exactly? Did that car have his name on it? No? Was there any evidence that suggests that he, or the Black Clovers, were even involved in the attack last night? No? Well then, it looks like it's your word against Daugherty's. Good luck proving any of that."

"We'll see."

As I stood up, the two thugs blocked my path.

"I didn't say you could go," Malone said.

"You didn't," I agreed, "but considering I have what you want, you're going to let me walk out of here alone without any trouble. Isn't that right, Malone?"

The two thugs looked at Malone, who thought for a moment before nodding his response. They slowly stepped aside.

"You gentlemen have a good afternoon," I said as I marched past them.

I turned and walked to the entrance, nodding to Berghoff on my way out. I'd gotten what I came for. Now, it was time to leave.

After buttoning my overcoat and heading out into the cold air, I casually headed down the block to retrieve my car from where I'd parked it. I couldn't shake the feeling that I was being followed the entire time.

CHAPTER 12

Hiding in the Spotlight

Shortly after leaving the Berghoff, I returned to my apartment—taking as many backroads as possible to lose whoever was following me. When convinced that I'd lost my tail, I headed upstairs. Checking every room in my apartment, I determined everything was just as I left it.

After hanging my coat and scarf up in the closet, I walked over to my desk and added the new information I'd gotten from Malone to my notebook. My visit to the Berghoff had been very productive. I now had a possible motive to charge Daugherty with arson and murder once I gathered more evidence. The drive-by didn't exactly have his name on it.

I quickly made a small sandwich (ham and cheese on sourdough) and reviewed my notes to ensure I included everything. It had been a risky move, letting Malone know I had the briefcase and blueprints, but it was sure to keep him focused on me instead of Harriet—at least, for the time being.

Part of me had been tempted to swing by Harriet's apartment to check up on her, but the lingering feeling of being followed made me think against it. Even though Daugherty believed that Hal was dead, I was willing to bet that he wasn't above kidnapping the dame who worked for him to squeeze as much information as he could from her.

I picked up the telephone and instructed the operator to connect me with her apartment. I breathed a sigh of relief when she answered.

"Hello?"

"It's me. I thought I'd give you a call and check in to see how you were doing."

"Clive?" There was excitement in her voice, "You have no idea how glad I am to hear your voice. I've been sitting in my apartment all day, doing absolutely nothing. I'm one crossword puzzle away from dying of boredom."

Despite her excitement, there was no hiding the restlessness in her voice. "It beats the alternative."

"I need to get out of my place," she said in a strained voice, "Couldn't you swing by and keep me company for a little while? I'm so lonely."

If I had a nickel for every lonely dame whose apartment I ended up in, I'd be able to afford a mansion twice the size of Daugherty's.

"I'm afraid not," the regret in my voice was genuine, "I think I'm being followed. It's too risky."

"What if I met you somewhere? I could get us a table in the Empire Dining Room at the Palmer House tonight..."

"No. Stay where you are. Right now, your apartment is the safest place for you."

"I can't stay here forever," she objected, "I'll go batty. There's nothing to do here."

The drastic change in her routine could not have been easy. In under twenty-four hours, Harriet Doyel had gone from a shining socialite lounge singer with her club to a woman who'd watched her world crumble before her eyes. Now, she couldn't leave her apartment on the off chance that Daugherty's goons might come looking for her. It's not an easy adjustment. Hopefully, when all this was over, she could still make an honest living as a lounge singer. Until then, she'd have to follow my rules to stay alive.

"I'm sorry. I know this isn't ideal, but it's only temporary. Once we find the people behind the attack last night and bring them to justice, you'll be free to leave your apartment whenever you like. But please ... for the time being, I need you to stay put. 'We can't keep you safe if we don't know where you are."

Maybe my logic was making too much sense for her, or maybe she'd just picked up a bad case of cabin fever after I left this morning; either way, she did not like the idea of staying in her apartment one bit.

"Fine..." she groaned, "I'll stay here." Her tone quickly changed to a more pleasant one, "You're lucky it's you who's asking me, otherwise, I'd be out the door already."

"Lucky me," I chuckled, "Listen, I still have a lot of work to do, but I promise, I'll call back soon. Don't do anything rash." Before she could object, I hung up.

I spent the next hour studying, sifting through my notebook, and making copies of the new information to put in the files I kept back at the office. Despite my valiant attempt to focus on the case outside the station, knowing Daugherty and his men were watching me like a hawk had me unusually tense. Usually, my nerves were as calm as steel in situations like this. For whatever reason, they now had me on the defensive.

To calm them, I poured myself a whiskey old-fashioned, with a touch more whiskey than I'd typically use. As an added precaution, I kept my revolver within arm's reach. If, by some miracle, Daugherty's men managed to follow me back home and were stupid enough to break down my door, I was going to be ready for them.

The next three hours passed like curdled milk dribbling out of its carton. Not a soul came knocking. The glowing embers of the dwindling cigarette wedged between my index and middle finger threatened to sear the skin, so I stamped the butt into the ashtray with the others and lit a fresh one.

When the telephone in the den rang, I answered it on the fourth bell, expecting to hear Harriet on the other line complaining about how bored she was again. To my surprise, the voice, instead, belonged to John Foster.

"Hill. It's Foster." His tone was strictly business. I had a feeling that whatever he was about to say next would not be good news. "After you left for the Berghoff, I sent Craig Lewis over to Miss Doyel's apartment in a patrol car, just like you asked. He's been watching the building and giving regular reports every hour."

You didn't need to be a gumshoe to see that John intentionally prolonged sharing the real reason he'd called. I'm not the kind of person who likes being kept waiting in anticipation. There was no time to sit back and play this game with him.

"If you're going to keep dancing around the issue, I'm going to need to put on my other shoes," I said with growing impatience, "Quit stalling and get to the point."

He sighed, frustrated, "About ten minutes ago, Lewis telephoned me from a callbox in the downtown area. He told me he saw Miss Doyel exit her building and enter a cab alone."

Damnit, Harriet, I cursed under my breath. It was the exact opposite of what I told her to do. I rubbed my temples to relieve the headache slowly building in my skull.

Foster continued, "He followed her cab to the Palmer House, where she got out and headed inside the hotel. He telephoned me soon after. I called you the moment Lewis hung up."

"Is there a reason he didn't go after her himself?"

"He was in uniform and didn't want to cause a scene." It wasn't a solid reason, but it was a reason, nonetheless. "Considering your close relationship with Miss Doyel, I thought she'd respond better to a friendly face showing up, instead of a uniformed officer."

"Probably a good call," I agreed, "Thanks for the heads up, John. I'm leaving now."

"Understood," Foster said, "Lewis is still on site waiting for you. Do you think you'll need additional backup?"

"I'll manage."

Foster chuckled briefly, "So much for your night off."

"Would've been interrupted one way or another. I'll drop you a line once I have her." I told him before I hung up.

My hat and overcoat were on seconds later as I hurried out my apartment door.

Later that hour, I pulled my car up to the Monroe Street entrance of the Palmer House Hotel, tossed the keys to the sharply dressed valet waiting outside, and watched him drive away to park it. After placing the ticket in my jacket pocket, I couldn't help but gaze up at the hotel's stunning architecture. The 25-story brick building had seen its fair share of rainy days over the years after being rebuilt three times. A few years back, the Palmer Family hired *Holabird & Roche* to design the building when it was rebuilt. Unlike the previous Palmer Hotel, the new building was a much larger facility than its predecessor, with grander and more lavish rooms for its guests.

The other valet was mildly confused when I started walking away from the hotel entrance but soon became too preoccupied with other arrivals to run after me.

Craig Lewis was standing at the corner of Monroe and Wabash under the steel girders of the elevated tracks. The rookie wore a navy-blue overcoat with five brass buttons on its front and a peaked cap. Matching gloves covered his hands. The neatly polished badge pinned to the outside of his coat was sure to draw plenty of unwanted attention.

He stood shivering in the cold air.

"Here you go, Lewis," I said, offering him a cigarette from the metal case in my pocket, "This should warm you up a bit."

The rookie waved his hand in protest. "I-I d-don't sm-m-smoke," he said through chattering teeth.

"I didn't ask you if you smoked. I offered you something to keep you from freezing out here. It's hard to understand you when you're teeth are chattering like the keys of a typewriter."

Before he could protest again, I shoved the cigarette past his lips and lit the tip with my lighter. He inhaled a lungful of warm tobacco smoke and held it in his chest for a moment. His shivering stopped.

"How's that?"

"Better..." he admitted, more clearly, as the smoke exited his lungs. His face turned green at the new sensation, but he took another puff of it a second later.

"Where's your car?"

Lewis pointed further down the street. "I parked it in an alley back there."

I quickly lit a cigarette for myself. "Any sign of Miss Doyel?"

He shook his head, "I've been watching both entrances since she went in. As far as I can tell, she's still inside."

"Good. I'll head in and look for her in the lobby. Knowing her, she'll most likely be in the Empire Dining Room if she's not there.

"You stay here and try and keep out of sight. We don't want anyone to get the wrong idea. This isn't an issue of *Dime Detective*. We're here to take Miss Doyel home, not start a gunfight. Do you understand?"

The rookie nodded again.

"Keep your eyes peeled for any suspicious characters," I warned, "If you get the feeling that things have gone south, you get to a phone and call for backup, then head inside. Do it exactly in that order. Not the other way around."

"How will I know when that happens?"

I stared at him, dumbfounded by his question. 'Didn't think my last statement required further explanation. "If you hear gunshots or see a large crowd of people running and screaming, I'd say it's safe to assume things went south."

"Ah ... yes," he said, slightly embarrassed, "That makes sense."

In truth, this was the first time the rookie had been anywhere without backup, let alone put in a situation that could turn into an active crime scene at the drop of a hat. Foster had assigned Lewis to watch Harriet's apartment alone because he expected it to be a simple stakeout. Nothing else. Of course, that was the plan until Harriet decided to sneak out for a quick night on the town. I could see the nervousness and inexperience in his eyes.

"You'll do fine," I patted his shoulder.

Having wasted enough time, I turned and walked back to the Palmer House alone.

The two-story lobby was as majestic and extravagant as the day the new building opened. It was a gilded vision of luxury, with accents of gold everywhere you looked. Hand-painted French murals and electric candelabras illuminated its walls in a way I can't even describe. The main staircase and large marble columns towered over the guests that occupied it. Unfortunately, Harriet was nowhere to be seen. Determined to find her, I continued into the Empire Dining Room.

Like the lobby, the Empire Room maintained the same golden décor you'd expect from an upscale place like the Palmer House. On the ceiling, gilded accents had been painted above the elegant chandeliers like regal crowns for each. It was spacious, with a sea of small tables covered in clean white tablecloths surrounding the stage and dance floor. Thick curtains hung over the windows and framed the stage. Simply put, the room was a work of art.

In the past year, the dining room had been converted into a supper club that quickly became the place to be for high-end entertainment. More than a few big names had graced its stage with their talents. On most nights, the regular entertainment, Richard Cole and his band performed on the stage for the guests; tonight was one such night.

As expected, the Empire Room was packed with guests when I entered. I waltzed over to where the dapper host was standing and gave him Harriet's description. The confusion on his face was not very reassuring. However, the mention of her name suddenly jogged his memory. He quickly nodded and pointed to a table marked *Reserved* near the edge of the dance floor, where Harriet sat alone.

She was wearing a navy dress with burgundy velvet accents and no back, which hugged the curves of her body like a lover. Her brunette hair had been styled to suggest this outing had been planned hours in advance. Being the music lover she was, her full attention was focused on the stage. She didn't notice me as I approached her table.

"I thought I told you to stay in your apartment," I said, pulling up a chair.

My sudden appearance startled her. "Clive, what are you doing here? How'd you even find me?"

"Call it a hunch." I had half a mind to take her by the wrist and drag her out of the place, but ultimately, I took a more subtle approach. "What in God's name possessed you to leave your apartment and come here alone?"

Harriet sighed, "I couldn't take another minute in my apartment. I had to get out."

"Not twenty-four hours ago, your club burned down and your bodyguard was gunned down in front of you," I reminded her, "Now, you're not even trying to hide." I grabbed her hand. "Let's get going before someone recognizes you."

At that moment, the spotlight shined on our table.

"Ladies and Gentlemen, this is an unexpected delight!" Richard Cole said into the microphone, "Tonight, we have Miss Harriet Doyel in our audience!"

The crowd cheered. I shook my head; it was the polar opposite of lying low. Now, Harriet was standing in the spotlight, with all eyes on her, serving herself on a silver platter for Daugherty and his goons. From where I stood, it looked like she was enjoying the attention.

"Would you do us the honor of gracing us with a song?"

Harriet smiled bashfully at her adoring public, entertaining the idea.

"I suppose," she said modestly, "Just one song."

The lounge singer walked across the dance floor and onto the stage. She whispered something in Cole's ear. He nodded and relayed the message to the band.

Cautiously, I sat back down and kept a close eye on each of the surrounding tables for any would-be kidnappers. Harriet stepped up to the mic like a bird in the sky. She nodded to the band, who began to play a rendition of *Between the Devil and the Deep Blue Sea*.

For a woman who'd lost almost everything, not an ounce of grief was heard in her angelic voice. She was back in her element. Her true passion. No one could scare her now.

Try as I might, getting a read on everyone in the room was impossible. In my experience, someone with ill intent usually has a tell before doing so, fidgeting in their seat, looking around nervously, or mapping out the closest possible exit. So far, no one there overtly struck me as a threat, but then again, if they were trying to avoid drawing attention to themselves, they were doing a perfect job blending in.

Out of the corner of my eye, I noticed a familiar face at one of the tables. I'd seen the same bag of bones at Hal's Place and the Bleeding Rose. The real question on my mind was, what was he doing here? Had he known Harriet would be there, or was this a happy coincidence? Based on the man's excited expression, I believed the latter.

As the song ended, Harriet basked in the applause her adoring public showered her with. The lounge singer took a humble bow before returning to her table. I shook my head disapprovingly. Sure, the performance had been enjoyable, but she'd carelessly exposed herself.

"We should get going," I suggested, "Let's hope Daugherty's goons didn't catch your little performance tonight. You may have painted a target on your back."

"That was beautiful," a voice behind me said.

"Show's over, bub," I warned, "Miss Doyel was just leaving."

When I turned to tell them off, I found myself face to face with the short, skinny man Harriet knew as Lenny Riggs.

Riggs glanced over at Harriet protectively, like a loyal mutt guarding its owner, "This guy bugging you, toots?" he growled.

The dame shook her head, "No. I'm fine, Lenny."

Riggs eased up slightly, but I noticed his jaw was still clenched.

"As I said, Miss Doyel and I are on our way out," I reiterated.

The thin bag of bones ignored me and invited himself to sit at the table with us. "Great performance, sweet cheeks. You're a real knockout."

Harriet blushed uncomfortably, "You're too kind." She diverted the topic of conversation back to him. "I'm glad to see you weren't at Hal's Place when it burned down last night."

"Looks like we both got lucky," he said, scooting closer to her. "I was waiting at my usual table for your performance.

"When they told everyone your first show was canceled because you were running late, I headed home."

I stared at the bony man.

"You were at Hal's Place last night, before the fire?" I asked, drawing my notepad and pencil from my pocket, "Mind if I ask you a couple of questions?"

The other man raised an eyebrow wearily at the question. His suspicion was all over his face. "What're you, a reporter, or something?"

Before I could come up with a lie on the spot, Harriet cut in.

"No. Clive—I mean, Detective Hill, is investigating the fire," she explained. "Any information you can give him would be a huge favor to me." She batted her eyelashes at him for added effect. That was more than enough to get Lenny Riggs to change his tune.

"Sure, doll. Anything for you."

"Approximately what time did you leave, Hal's Place last night?" I asked.

"Around seven-twenty, or so."

I began collecting his statement on a fresh page in my notebook. "While you were waiting for the show to begin, did you notice anything out of the ordinary—maybe a couple of new faces, or suspicious-looking people poking around where they shouldn't have?" I inquired.

Lenny thought momentarily, "Now that you mention it, I did pass a group of dodgy-looking fellas on my way out. At least five or six of them. Definitely no more than eight."

We were getting somewhere. "Could you give me a description of any of them? Maybe the clothes they were wearing? Anything that stood out to you."

"Well," he started, "they were wearing black coats, with black suits, and wide-brimmed hats. One or two of them were wearing charcoal-grey scarves around their necks. The one I nearly bumped into, had a lapel pin on the collar of his jacket, with an odd-looking symbol on it."

I could feel my pulse quicken, eager to uncover the identity of the strangers Riggs had encountered. "What kind of symbol?"

"A black four-leaf clover. Kinda a little early to celebrate Saint Patty's Day, if you ask me."

"The Black Clovers," I surmised, "Did you overhear anything they were talking about?"

"I didn't hear much," Riggs admitted, "Though, one of them did mention the name, '*Daugherty*' and something a mansion, but nothing else."

After writing down the new information, I looked at him again, "One last question: where did you go after leaving Hal's Place?"

"Me?" he asked, confused. His tone became more defensive, "I don't have to tell you! That's none of your business!"

I frowned. "A man was gunned down in front of a burning building filled with innocent people. The very same building you visited, before it went up in flames." The coldness in my eyes conveyed just how serious I was. "So, I'm making it my business."

There was a hint of fear in the man's eyes. Riggs nervously glanced back and forth between Harriet and me.

"Y-You don't think *I* had something to do with it?"

"Answer the question, Mr. Riggs," I repeated slowly, emphasizing my words, "Where did you go?"

He eventually caved under the pressure. "I walked a few blocks and found myself a pro skirt! All Right! Then went home!" His cheeks went bright red as he looked at Harriet, pleading apologetically with his eyes. "It was a one-time thing! Honest! She meant nothing to me! You're the only dame for me!"

Harriet didn't seem to share the sentiment, but she made sure Riggs didn't get wise about her feelings.

As much as I enjoyed watching Riggs tread water, I needed more facts.

"What was her name?"

"What?"

"What was the name of the woman you were barney-mugging?" I repeated, "I'd like to follow up with her and see if your story checks out with hers?"

His face flushed red with exasperation and embarrassment. "Christ! I didn't get her name! We played hanky-panky, then went our separate ways!"

As far as alibies went, his was as flimsy as a wet paper bag—though, honestly, I wasn't about to set off on a wild goose chase to find some random dame just to confirm his story. I felt dirty even picturing the deed in my head.

"I'll ... take your word for it then," I let my gaze drop to my watch. It was only then that I realized how late it was getting. "Thank you for your cooperation, Mr. Riggs. Unfortunately, Miss Doyel and I have somewhere we need to be. If you remember anything else about last night, you can reach me in my office at the police station on 11th and State Street.

"If I'm not in, for whatever reason, feel free to leave your information with my secretary. She'll be sure to pass it along to me."

Harriet and I stood up and started walking toward the exit. Our departure didn't stop Riggs from trying to follow us.

"Where are you off to in such a hurry?" he pried.

"Nothing you need to concern yourself with," I said as politely as I could manage, "Good evening, Mr. Riggs."

The two of us quickly made for the crowded lobby, leaving the confused man alone with no clues about where we were going. We grabbed our coats and headed out. Instead of taking the Monroe Street entrance, I led Harriet through the other door on South Wabash Avenue. Once outside, we met with Craig Lewis, who was right where I'd left him.

"Harriet, this is Officer Lewis. He works with me at the station." The brunette gave a quick *'Hello'* before I continued, "He's going to give you a lift back to your apartment for me and stay with you until I get back."

The news shocked the young woman. "Wait ... Where are you going?"

As much as I wanted to tell her, it was too dangerous. "The less you know, the safer you'll be. Trust me."

I leaned in close next to Lewis's ear.

"Get her home. Take all the back roads in case you're followed." The rookie nodded his understanding. "Head upstairs with her. Lock the door, and don't open it for anyone who isn't me. Understand?" He nodded again.

Satisfied with his answers, I turned to Harriet. "Officer Lewis will keep you safe," I assured her, "I'll swing by your apartment once I've finished up. This time, stay put."

It wasn't the most romantic goodbye I've ever given, but it was straight and to the point. The clock was ticking. The sooner I got Harriet off the streets, the safer she'd be.

Lewis gave her a light tug in the opposite direction. "Come along, Miss Doyel. We should get going."

Her eyes protested, but her body obeyed the officer's suggestion. She'd be safe with Lewis until I got back. Lewis was one of a handful of cops that had my complete trust. He wouldn't let me down.

Before I let myself linger, I turned and headed back toward the Monroe entrance. When I arrived, I handed the valet my ticket and watched him telephone the garage to bring the car around. A few minutes later, another valet pulled my car up to the curb and exited the driver's door while the engine was still running.

After pulling away from the Palmer House, I switched on the radio. President Roosevelt was giving his State of the Union Address, but I didn't hear much of it. What I did hear however, was the *click* of a loaded pistol and a familiar voice in the back seat.

"Drive, copper," said Malone, "You and I are going to take a little ride."

We drove for several minutes before I was instructed to pull the car over when we were in a more secluded part of the city. Before I could open my mouth to ask where we were, I felt hard metal smack the back of my head. The next thing I knew, the world went black.

CHAPTER 13

At the Light's Edge

I woke up in a dark room with no idea where I was—it could've been a warehouse or a basement—your guess is as good as mine. For the most part, the room was shrouded in darkness, except for a single overhead light with a metal shade, which hung a few feet above me.

As the groggy world slowly came back into focus, I found myself tied to a chair. After failing to wiggle free from my bonds, I heard a wicked chuckle from somewhere in the surrounding darkness.

"Good evening, detective," Malone said, "Glad to see you're finally awake."

Malone stepped out from the shadows and into the light. There was a lit cigarette tucked in the corner of his mouth. He blew some smoke in my direction.

"I'm sure you know what you're doing here." I had a few good guesses. "Seeing that you asked me plenty of questions earlier today, I think it's only fair I get to ask you a couple of my own. If you refuse to answer any of my questions, these fine gentlemen are going to make things very uncomfortable for you."

As if on cue, two husky men, who I hardly would've described as "*gentle*," made themselves known at the light's edge. The brims of their hats cast dark shadows over their faces, making it hard to identify them from where I was sitting.

I was sure of two things at that moment: I was in for a considerable amount of pain, and whatever these thugs dished out, they were going to keep me alive until I told them what they wanted to know. After that, I was as good as dead.

Malone dragged a chair over from the shadows and sat comfortably in it. The cocksure businessman was under the impression that I was just going to hand him what he wanted. I was neither impressed nor intimidated by his efforts.

"Now that you understand the situation, 'mind telling me how you know so much about Mr. Daugherty and his business?"

I shrugged. "I'm a detective. It's my job to keep an eye on every notable low-life in this city. Your boss is getting sloppy ... or have you been the one calling the shots?"

The smile on his face soured. He nodded to the nearby thugs. The larger of the two stepped in front of me while the other took his position behind me and made sure the chair remained in place—how kind of my host to make sure that I didn't suffer a concussion if my chair toppled over. I was met with a forceful punch to the stomach; my body lurched from the impact.

"Come now, there's no need to get personal. I'd hoped to keep things civilized."

Once I finished coughing, Malone proceeded with his next question.

"Who gave you the blueprints for Mr. Daugherty's casino?"

"No one," I grunted.

A second fist collided with my stomach. I hadn't lied, but anything I said that wasn't what Malone wanted to hear would only be seen as an act of defiance in his eyes.

"Who gave you the blueprints?" he repeated.

"No one."

A firm fist made contact with the side of my face. For a moment, I saw stars.

"Easy on the face," Malone warned the thug playing the chin music, "I still need him to talk. He can't do that if his jaw's broken."

Using my tongue, I dapped at my sore lip and tasted a few droplets of blood on it, but nothing major. My stomach, on the other hand, was quickly becoming a light shade of purple. I wasn't given much time to analyze the pain further as Malone fired another question.

"Did Lawrence give you Mr. Daugherty's books and blueprints the night he died?"

I kept my mouth closed and glared at him defiantly. When I didn't answer, the assault on my stomach and torso continued.

"What did you do with them?" he demanded, "Where are they?"

All the breath escaped my lungs. Even if I had air left in them, I still wouldn't have said a thing. My silence was driving him crazy. It was a small victory, but one that made a noticeable difference. I was getting to them.

My thoughts drifted to Harriet. Every fist pounding my body kept Daugherty's attention on me and not her. Despite her strong will and ability to deal with men like Malone, I doubted she would've lasted long in a situation like this once the pain started. With any luck, she was back in her apartment with Lewis protecting her, far away from Daugherty and his goons.

The muscle pounding his fists against my body was starting to work up a sweat from the intensity of the beating. Malone was gradually losing his cool. Every time I refused to answer his question, his growing desperation became more difficult to hide with each passing moment. By the time he'd finished yelling, his voice raw, the thug hitting me was panting from exhaustion. It was clear that he needed a breather.

Once Malone had collected himself enough to notice the winded expression on the man's face, he motioned for him to stop his attack.

"That's enough, Angus. Take five." Malone pointed at the thug behind me. "Rory, you take over for a while."

Rory did as he was told. Despite his frustration, Malone was noticeably impressed by my resilience.

"You're a hard man to break, detective," he admitted, "Not many men can take a beating like that and keep their mouth shut. You're one tough son of a bitch, I'll give you that. Just tell me what I want to know and I'll make all your pain go away."

The room and everything in it began fading in and out of focus. It was getting difficult to hold my head up. The thug

Malone called "Angus" grabbed a fistful of my hair and pulled it to keep my eyes focused on Malone.

"Mr. Daugherty's going to get his belongings one way or another, so just tell us where they are and we'll take care of the rest."

I looked at the blurring image of the man before me and opened my mouth. The air I summoned to my lungs felt like sharp pins puncturing them as I inhaled. Still, I mustered enough strength to form one word:

"No..."

My voice was barely audible, but it had been loud enough for the gutter prince to hear. He stood there seething.

In a fit of rage, Malone kicked my chair backward. The sudden outburst had caught the giant thug by surprise as he failed to keep the chair I was tied to level. Before he could react, my head struck him square in the stomach. He involuntarily clutched his gut and doubled over in response, causing the chair to land on the floor with me still in it.

I suddenly felt my right arm come loose from the rope—though I didn't let it stray too far from where it had been bound—and discovered I could slip it in and out with minimum difficulty. Instead of trying to free myself with my liberated arm, I closed my eyes and feigned unconsciousness while listening intently to what was said next.

"Son of a bitch!" Malone shouted; I could hear him pacing back and forth as he huffed angrily, "We searched this city up and down and had nothing to show for it! If we don't find out where this bastard is hiding the boss's property, it'll be your necks and mine!

"He has a meeting with the bank to buy the site for his casino on Saturday! You know as well as I do that the bank won't sell him anything until they've seen the plans and his ledgers!"

"What if Lawrence already passed the boss's stuff along to Hal?" Rory speculated.

"Thinking isn't your strong suit, is it, Rory," Malone retorted. "The boys didn't find them when they cracked open Hal's safe a few hours ago. The only thing in there was a few stacks of cash—which they divided up among themselves—but nothing else. The first thing a man like Hal would've done after getting something as valuable as that is put it in his safe and lock it away. Since they didn't turn up there, that means he never had them."

"Then, where are they?"

"No idea," Malone sneered, "but, I got a feeling the dick knows exactly where to find them. There's no way he'd be playing hardball like this if he didn't already know where the items Lawrence took were. I wager he still has them."

"You want one of us to give Shifty and his crew a call, have them search his pad 'til they find the stuff?" Angus asked.

"Nah. The boss has Shifty and his crew working another job tonight. Strictly need to know—you get what I'm saying? Hopefully, he gets it done this time. He's already on thin ice with the boss as it is..."

Malone suddenly remembered I was still there and let out an exhausted sigh.

"...Get the dick up. 'Break's over."

I felt strong hands lift my chair and set it upright. Another hand lightly slapped my cheek twice to wake me.

"Don't go nodding off on us now, copper," Malone instructed, "We're not done with you yet..."

My eyes opened slowly. Behind my back, I carefully wiggled my right arm until it slid free of the rope. I kept it in position to maintain the illusion that it was still bound.

Rory had a thin knife drawn. Its blade looked razor sharp.

"Since you don't want to do this the easy way, we're gonna try something else..." Malone said. He gestured to Rory. "Rory, here, is gonna start cutting until you tell us where Mr. Daugherty's belongings are. Before we start, is there anything you want to come clean about?"

When I didn't respond, Malone gave another sigh of disapproval.

"Have it your way then."

The shorter thug approached me with the knife held at eye level. The man ran the edge of it across my cheek and applied a small amount of pressure against the skin. I winced in pain as the sharp knife sliced the flesh, causing a small trickle of blood to run down it.

"Ready to talk?" Malone taunted.

I shook my head.

"Very well. Continue."

The thug lowered the knife and began trailing it across my chest.

In a flash, I jerked my arm free, grabbed the man's knife hand, and thrust it into his throat. The startled man collapsed on the ground, gurgling and clutching at the open wound as blood poured from it. A moment later, his body went limp.

Malone and the taller goon stood momentarily stunned by how quickly Rory had been dispatched—a moment was all I needed.

During that time, I had untied myself and gotten to my feet. Before either of them could react, I charged Malone and drove the knife deep into his right thigh.

Malone howled in pain as he gingerly tried to pull the sharp object from his leg, eventually giving up and dropping to his other knee.

The thug rushed over to help Malone, but the fuming man shook his head and pointed at me.

"Don't just stand there you numbskull! After him!"

It was nothing short of a miracle that I'd been able to perform the feat I had a moment ago. I ran solely on adrenaline, but I knew that would only last for so long. If I was going to get out of this with my life, I needed to put as much distance as I could between me and the bellowing thug chasing me.

Patting my jacket, I was surprised to find that my captors had left my revolver in its holster. It seemed they thought the tight knots that had bound me to the chair would be enough to ensure I didn't use it. It had been a sloppy mistake that had cost them dearly.

I quickly drew my weapon and fired blindly behind me at my pursuer as I ran. There was a grunt of pain and a loud *thud*—but I didn't dare look back to see if I was still being followed. Instead, I continued up a flight of stairs, through another door, and into the night air.

I didn't have time to stop and get my bearings. Doing so would've only slowed me down. The pain was beginning to return. I knew I wouldn't get far on foot in my condition. What I needed was a set of wheels.

As if an answer to my prayer, I spotted my car parked a few feet from the building. Once I reached it, I fumbled around my pockets, searching for my keys. Unfortunately, it seemed that Malone had kept them after knocking me out.

With no alternative, I thrust my elbow against the driver-side window. The glass shattered into pieces. I unlocked the door and climbed inside as soon as it was clear. Feeling under the steering wheel, I grabbed two of the wires and touched them together until the engine roared to life.

Flooring the gas pedal, I sped away, leaving Malone and the building he'd kept me in far behind me.

A short time later, I was back in the city, only to find myself in another pickle. As I attempted to slow my speed by pressing the brake pedal, I found that the line had been cut. Like it or not, my vehicle would not stop on its own.

Honking my horns in loud bursts, I attempted to warn the other cars around me of my peril. Some moved out of the way, while others were not so fortunate. Unable to stop, I drove through several red lights, barely missing the oncoming traffic.

I heard police sirens and saw flashing lights in my rearview mirror. A couple of cop cars were racing after me.

"Pull over to the curb!" I heard an officer say over the speaker, "I repeat; pull over to the curb!"

As much as I would've loved to cooperate, my car had other ideas. Dodging cars like a madman, I attempted to turn onto the least populated streets to limit the possible casualties. The squad cars followed close behind.

"This is your last warning. Pull over to the curb, or we will use deadly force."

As terrible as that option sounded, a worse one was fast approaching—I was running out of road. My car was careening toward the river. I could do little as it crashed through the stone railing and dove into the frozen water.

My forehead suddenly slammed against the steering wheel before I knew what happened.

CHAPTER 14

A Cold Awakening

When I woke up, I was underwater. My car was fully submerged and sinking to the bottom of the Chicago River. It was late, and the waters were dark. The only light giving me some limited visibility in the murky water came from my car's headlights, but they quickly flickered out. It reached the bottom in seconds and settled on the muddy river floor.

I quickly swam through the shattered driver's side window and evacuated my wreck. Once out of my sunken vehicle, I searched for my next exit. While I knew the break in the ice could not have been far from where my car went in, the bump to my head had disoriented me.

My lungs were on fire. Aside from the burning pain from my injuries, they ached for another breath of air. My heart rate quickened as the cold water filled every nerve in my skin with a burning chill. I needed to get out of the water as soon as possible.

Pushing off the river floor, I swam upward, kicking my legs to hasten my speed. My throbbing head had the world spinning. I was swimming blind. If I didn't find the opening in the ice, I'd quite literally be sleeping with the fishes. Soon, I reached the thick sheet above me, only to realize that I'd drifted away from my mark. Panic set in as the air in my lungs screamed for release.

A moment later, something on the other side of the ice illuminated the sleek surface. I could hear muffled shouting but couldn't make sense of any of it. The light trailed over to a nearby section of the ice. As my eyes followed it and the world finally stopped spinning, I found the exit five feet from my position.

My joints were quickly becoming stiffer as I swam toward it. The cold water made five feet feel like a hundred. It numbed my hands and feet, making my strokes and kicks slow and heavy. With every fiber of my being, I swam to the opening as my vision began to tunnel.

I gasped a copious amount of air the second my head poked out of the water's surface. Grasping the frosty sides of the ice edge, I did my best to control my breathing. Before losing all feeling in my arms, I pulled myself out of the water with my remaining strength until I was flat on my stomach across the ice. The waterlogged jacket felt heavy on my exhausted body as I slowly crawled toward the shore.

"Over there!" someone shouted, "On the ice!"

When I finally reached the dock, a group of strangers was waiting to help me to safety. I was quickly led inside the bridge house by some workers and set in front of a warm stove. Once out of the cold, I stripped my drenched clothes off and wrapped myself in a wool blanket. One of the men offered me a steaming beverage from the kettle on the stove, which I graciously accepted.

The two cops who'd witnessed the incident joined us in the bridge house, fully prepared to arrest me. When I identified myself as a detective and explained the situation, they found someone to stitch up the cut on my cheek and torso (which, if I'm being honest, wasn't the cleanest sewing job, but it was better than nothing). Once my other wounds had been tended to, they left me alone to thaw out in peace.

Pulling my notebook out of my pocket, I discovered its pages were soaked and sticking together—though I knew they would dry out, I couldn't help but wonder how legible they'd be when they did. Thankfully, I'd had the good sense to copy most of the notes for the case file if something like this happened.

Eventually, John Foster arrived on the scene with a dry set of clothes.

"A little cold for a nighttime swim, wouldn't you say?" he teased, "I'm told you were one carrot short of being a frostbitten snowman." When his attempt at humor didn't land, he coughed uncomfortably, "I ... uh ... brought you some fresh clothes. Get changed. I'll give you a lift back to the station."

After getting dressed, Foster helped me out to his car. I fished my lighter and cigarette case out of the pockets of my wet clothes. Fortunately, the contents of the metal case were dry enough to use. My lighter, on the other hand, was a different story. I struggled to get a flame for a few minutes before tossing it to the curb.

Noticing my frustration, John drew his own and lit the tip of the cigarette in my mouth.

"Here. Let me."

I didn't protest as the warm air filled my lungs. Breathing, in general, was painful, and the sensation of smoke in my lungs caused me to cough heavily.

"How are you feeling?"

"Like hell," I admitted, attempting to hide my pain, "...but better."

"You look like hell," he agreed, stating the obvious, "Don't tell me this is all from the accident."

I shook my head. "Malone was waiting to ambush me in my car at the Palmer House. The next thing I know, I'm waking up in a dark warehouse tied to a chair. Malone wanted to know where Lawrence hid the books and blueprint he'd stolen. When I didn't tell him, he had his thugs try to beat the answers out of me."

Foster raised an eyebrow. "Did it work?"

I shot him a look suggesting how ridiculous he was for asking. "What do you think?"

"No. You're too much of a stubborn son of a bitch to break that easily," he chuckled, "How'd you manage to get away?"

"Some details are better left unsaid," I told him, not proud of the violent actions I'd been forced to take to ensure my escape. "But once I dealt with Malone and his muscle, I made it outside, found my car, and hailed tail out of there. I didn't realize they'd cut my breaks until I was already back in the city. By then, it was too late to do anything."

To illustrate this, I glanced out the passenger side window at the destruction. From how things looked, my runaway car had left a sizable trail of wreckage in its wake—it was a wonder that I hadn't been arrested. Although I'd done everything possible to minimize the damage, it was still quite a mess.

A line of smashed cars occupied the street, many with deep dents on various sides of the vehicles. Broken glass and metal parts littered the pavement. The police had effectively closed down the roads and controlled the gathering crowds. They were far enough from our car that they couldn't see me, but that didn't keep me from wrestling with my guilt.

"How many were injured?" I asked, afraid of the answer.

Foster shifted in his seat, "More than a couple of citizens with minor cuts and bruises, one or two with broken bones, but nothing a few days rest can't fix."

If that was the case, everyone, including myself, had been fortunate—though, I wouldn't put it past John to keep the number of casualties from me to ease my conscience. I decided that was probably for the best.

"You hear back from Lewis?" I asked, casually changing the subject as we pulled away.

John shook his head. "Not yet. Why?"

I blinked, "He was supposed to call you the moment he and Harriet got back to her apartment."

"Now, let's not jump to any conclusions," John said, though the hint of concern in his voice betrayed the calm face he was putting on, "Maybe Lewis just had his hands full with Miss Doyel and it slipped his mind. It wouldn't be the first time one of our officers forgot to call in while babysitting a beautiful dame."

Not the rookie. Craig Lewis would've called in while the world was on fire if there was something to report. No. He would've called once he was certain Harriet was safe—unless she wasn't. A chilling fear gripped my heart. Something wasn't right.

Just then, I spotted a telephone booth on the next street corner.

"Stop the car. Pull over here." I said before hopping out of the car and hurrying to the pay phone. I frantically checked my pockets for loose change but didn't find any. I turned to John, "Can you spot me a nickel?"

He flipped me a shiny coin, which I caught with minimum effort.

I dropped the nickel in the slot and asked the operator to connect me to Harriet's apartment. The line continued to ring with no response. A bad feeling crept into my gut—it was more than just my bruised anatomy talking to me.

"Any luck?"

I shook my head, "No one's answering."

"Do you know the way to her building from here?"

Giving a nod, I jumped into the passenger seat. Before I could say "drive," the tires squealed, and the car sped down the street.

Shortly after arriving, John and I climbed the stairs until we reached Harriet's apartment. As we approached, it became clear that things were out of sorts. What was most alarming was seeing the apartment door knocked off its hinges and lying on the carpet. The broken security chain dangled against the door frame.

Having no idea what we were walking into, we drew our weapons and held them at the ready as we entered. I took the lead while Foster followed closely behind.

It wasn't long before we noticed two bodies slumped over in unnatural poses on the floor. Both were male (much to my relief). One of them had demolished the cocktail table when he collapsed. The other was sprawled out with a bullet wound to the throat—the loose hand beneath his jugular suggested that he had not died immediately. Through the copious amount of blood soiling his jacket, I could faintly make out the outline of the lapel pin on his collar.

"The Black Clovers," I whispered.

Judging by the series of bullet holes in the wall and the weapons they'd been holding, there was no denying that both men had died in a gunfight.

We found two more stiffs in the hallway leading to Harriet's bedroom. A chill ran down my spine as I peered into the lifeless eyes of one of the men—wide open and frozen in an expression of shock (no doubt due to the gaping hole in his forehead).

My pulse quickened. Daugherty had sent these men to find Harriet. How had he known where she was? Had they followed her home from the Palmer House? More questions flooded my mind.

I hurried forward to the dark bedroom door, which was wide open. Everything inside of me wanted to call out her name—just to know she was alive—but I didn't know if any of her attackers were still there. Using the outer wall as cover, I poked around the doorway.

My heart dropped.

Craig Lewis lay motionless on the floor with several bullet wounds in his chest. His pistol was on the ground beside his limp body. His blood had soaked into the carpet, creating a shallow puddle of crimson. A pang of grief tugged at my insides. I'd sent him to his death.

I shook those thoughts away. There was still a job to do. Lowering my guard now, even to mourn a fallen colleague, would lead me to a similar fate if I didn't stay sharp.

Looking further into the room, I noticed another body on the floor. Even in the darkness, I recognized his scarred face: *Shifty Shane Griffin.*

Through the light of the window, I could see fresh wounds across his already-marred face. Deep lines of crimson raked through the skin on his cheek as if a giant cat had clawed him. There had been a struggle.

As I turned around, I found Harriet Doyel, very much alive, curled up against the wall like a frightened child, panting heavily, with a pistol pointed in front of her. The young woman must have still been in shock because she didn't respond when I called her name the first time. Her wide eyes were frozen in a fixed position on the spot where her attacker had been standing.

Carefully stepping out of her line of fire, I was determined to bring her around.

"Harriet..." I said, crouching near her so she could see me. Cautiously, I reached out and removed the pistol from her trembling hands.

She'd been through yet another horrific ordeal. As if the events of last night had not been traumatic enough for her, the fact that Daugherty had ordered a squad of his armed goons to break into her apartment to kidnap her was more than she could bear. Harriet was terrified.

"Are you hurt?"

She subtly shook her head but kept her petrified eyes locked on the ghost of her attacker. They grew more and more distant as her mind began to shut down. She was a prisoner of her fears.

At that moment, Foster entered the bedroom and flipped on the light with his elbow. He immediately noticed Lewis's body.

"What the Hell happened here?" he asked, almost accusingly.

In Harriet's vulnerable state, demanding that she relive the terrifying event before she was ready would only prove counterproductive. If we pushed too hard, we'd risk her retreating into herself further. While I admired John's passion, we would not get the answers we needed with him shouting at her.

"Not now," I told him, "Get the station on the phone. Tell them to get over here immediately."

At first, it looked like he wanted to argue, but he quickly nodded instead, then grabbed the telephone on the nightstand.

I turned my attention back to Harriet.

"It'll be all right," I assured her, "You're safe now."

"Clive?" she asked as if it was the first time she'd realized I was there.

I removed my jacket (not an easy task to complete with my bruised body) and wrapped it around her to keep her warm. The life in her eyes was slowly returning. To keep her from backtracking, I made sure to keep Harriet's attention focused on me and not the bloody bodies scattered about her apartment.

"Can you stand?" I asked. She nodded.

I could tell she was tempted to look at the bodies.

"You don't need to see this. Just keep your eyes on me. You're safe."

Her eyes met mine. Tears were beginning to form in them. She was barely able to keep herself together.

"Why don't the two of us step out into the hallway and just talk? How does that sound?"

The trembling brunette nodded.

Helping her to her feet, we maintained eye contact the whole time.

"All right, Harriet, I need you to trust me. Listen to me carefully. First, I need you to close your eyes." She did as she was told. "Good. Now reach out and take my hand..."

A second later, her delicate hand was wrapped in mine.

"I'm going to guide you out of here. I know it's hard, but I'm going to need you to keep your eyes closed until I tell you it's safe to open them."

She nodded again.

For the next few minutes, I led Harriet by the hand through the hallway and carefully guided her footsteps around the fallen bodies and puddles of blood until we found ourselves in the outer hallway. To my surprise, she kept her eyes closed the entire journey.

"All right," I told her once the horrific scene was out of view, "You can open your eyes now."

Her eyelids fluttered open like the wings of a butterfly. She threw her arms around me and squeezed tightly when she saw me—the unexpected gesture—while pleasant—was painful for my battered body. I winced reflexively and let out a pained groan.

The sound made Harriet break the embrace.

"What is it? What's wrong? Did I hurt you?"

I lovingly removed her hands from my chest but continued to hold them.

"No," I said, "Just a little banged up. Not your fault. My chest's still a little tender from the beating it took. That's all."

"Oh, Clive ... You are hurt."

The concern on her face made me smile. After everything she'd gone through in the past forty-eight hours, Harriet was still worried about me.

"I'll be fine," I said, putting on a brave face, "It's not the first time I've been a punching bag."

At that moment, the cut on my chest started bleeding again. It wasn't life-threatening, but I felt the blood soak through the clean white fabric. The sutures had come undone. Given how hastily they'd been done, it was entirely possible they hadn't been done right from the start.

"You're bleeding!" Harriet gasped, pointing out the line of crimson in the white fabric.

Damn it, I thought, *this was a clean shirt.* I'd have to find another clean one in my size once we returned to the station. As if the poor girl hadn't seen enough blood tonight.

"So I am," I agreed.

"Who did this to you?"

I shrugged, "Just a couple of Daugherty's thugs trying to find out where Lawrence's briefcase is. You can imagine how upset they were when I didn't talk."

This did nothing to slow Harriet's worrying. She stepped closer and delicately inspected the sewn cut on my cheek.

"Your poor face ... They did this to you?" I nodded. Her soft fingers trailed over to the bruise on my forehead, "... And this too?"

"No..." I admitted hesitantly, "That one's from the car accident."

The young woman's jaw dropped. "A car accident?" By this time, my pain was doing a great job of distracting Harriet from her own. Her fears were entirely focused on my well-being.

"I'll be fine. Honestly. It looks worse than it is," I lied.

Tears slid down her cheeks. "Oh, Clive... This is all my fault. If I hadn't left my apartment—"

"If you start telling yourself what you could've done differently, you're only going to dig up more regret. Looks like you've got enough already." I stated. "Thinking about that's a lost cause. The ink is already dry on that page in the story. What you can do, though, is tell me what happened here tonight."

The brunette debated whether or not she wanted to relive the terrible events she'd witnessed. I didn't blame her, but I wasn't going to get a statement from any of the dead men in her apartment, so her story was all I had to go off of.

"I realize this is hard for you," my voice was full of understanding, "but there's a dead cop in there. A friend and colleague. The moment Daugherty killed him, he made this personal. You may not be ready to talk about what happened tonight, but I'm not going to be able to nail this son of a bitch until you tell me."

Harriet did her best to compose herself. There were still tears in her eyes, but her voice was calm enough to understand.

"Once we left the Palmer House, your friend took me back to my apartment and locked the front door as soon as we got inside. He told me to wait in the den while he searched every room. A little while later, he joined me on the sofa. We talked for a bit—I did most of it—but it was enjoyable. He seemed like a nice guy.

"About an hour after we got back—around eight-thirty, maybe nine o'clock, I can't remember the exact time — we heard footsteps in the hallway. Your friend went to the door and looked through the peephole to see who was there. When he realized it wasn't you, he told me to keep quiet and barricade myself in the bedroom. I did as he said. I grabbed the pistol from the nightstand's top drawer beside my bed.

"Someone was pounding on the front door; they kept pounding until they finally kicked it in. After that, I heard a lot of shooting in the other room. It was loud! I was so frightened!"

She paused for a moment to calm herself before continuing.

"Your friend ... he was very brave. Even after getting wounded, he was still putting up a fight. I'm sure you would've been proud. If he hadn't been here ... I don't know what would've happened."

It gave me some small comfort knowing that Lewis had died putting up a brave fight to keep Harriet safe. Still,

Daugherty had killed him in his selfish conquest. I'd personally make sure he answered for his crimes.

"What happened next?"

Harriet shivered as if she were waking up to a cold chill. "That man—the other man you saw—killed him and stepped over his body like it was nothing. H-He told me I was coming with him. When I refused, he tried to grab me ... I scratched his face..."

The tears poured from her eyes.

"It-It all happened so fast ... The pistol was in my hand ... I-I didn't know what else to do..."

"It was self-defense," I told her calmly, "You did what you had to."

Harriet was still at odds with herself. "I-I never killed anyone before. Gus never had to kill anyone while he was pretending to be me. One look at him was enough to scare them into behaving. There was no need for killing." The gravity of the situation was weighing on her. "I killed someone..." she sobbed, "I'm just as bad as those men in my apartment!"

I took her by the shoulders and forced her to look at me.

"Don't you say that! Don't even think that! Those men were hired killers. They killed for money. You didn't have a choice—and I know you didn't enjoy doing it.

"Listen to me carefully. You are not a bad person, Harriet. You've been through a lot. More than most. But that does not make you a bad person at all.

"Cyrus Daugherty is a heartless bastard who doesn't give a damn about all the good people he kills to get what he wants. Everyone is expendable to him, including his men. It's all just business to him.

"You're not like that. You have a kind heart. You care deeply for the people around you. Your fans. The people who visited your club. The men who worked for you. I know that if the roles had been reversed last night, Daugherty would not have batted an eye as he watched an entire building of innocent people go up in flames, or his men get gunned down in front of him.

"You. Mourned. Them. All.

"Don't you throw your hat in the same ring as Daugherty or any of the idiots he sent after you tonight! You are better."

I could see that my speech had gotten through to her. Every word of it had been taken to heart.

Before she could say anything, I pulled her in close and kissed her passionately. All the tension in her body dissolved into the kiss. I didn't even feel the pain plaguing mine while our lips touched.

I've kissed a lot of dames over the years. None that I would say I truly cared about. It was always more of an expected formality to propel things toward other nightly activities. It was empty. A con to satisfy carnal pleasures. Nothing more. But that kiss ... that was something different. It was almost spiritual. A simple action, fueled by our shared affection for each other, that seemed to say everything that our words could not.

A forced cough interrupted the moment.

Harriet and I opened our eyes and spotted John standing in the doorway, watching us smugly. I knew him well enough to decipher his thinking: *You sly dog.*

"Sorry to interrupt," he apologized, the half-smile still on his face, "I just got off the phone with Captain Shoemaker.

He's sending some cars over with the coroner to snap some pictures of the crime scene before the press catch a whiff of what happened here tonight. Once we finish up, I'll give you both a lift back to the station so we can figure out what to do next."

CHAPTER 15

A Snowy Sanctuary

Harriet seemed like her usual self once we got back to headquarters. After wrapping the singer in a blanket, Dolores brought a fresh pot of joe to help warm us. John and I kept our coffee black. Harriet's, however, was more cream than coffee. It seemed the change of scenery and hot beverage had improved her mood considerably.

After searching my entire office for an extra shirt to change into, I couldn't find any. Fortunately, John had a pair of clean clothes in his closet that he graciously lent me. Though we weren't the same size, the shirt fit well enough. I promised not to bloody it up too much while it was in my possession, but judging by how the night had gone, there was no telling whether I could keep that promise.

While Dolores dropped my shirt off at the cleaners, the three of us gathered in my office and listened to Harriet give her statement about the attempted kidnapping—which matched up with the story she'd given me. For obvious reasons, it wasn't safe to have Harriet return to her apartment (or mine, for that matter) until all this had blown over.

"Where am I supposed to go?" Harriet whined, "Do you expect me to sleep in my car tonight? This cold weather will murder my voice."

"Calm down, Miss Doyel," John said, trying to get a handle on the situation. "You're not going to spend the night in your car. I've spoken to Captain Shoemaker, and he's arranged for you to stay in a hotel for a few days. It won't be the Ritz, but you'll have a roof over your head and a warm place to sleep.

John held up a sealed envelope. "The name of the hotel is enclosed in this envelope. The captain wants to limit the number of people who know the exact address. Even I don't know where you'll be staying."

"I'll be all alone?" Harriet asked, "What happens if the Black Clovers find me? How are you going to keep me safe if none of you know where I'll be?"

"You won't be alone. Detective Hill will be going with you." He handed the envelope to me. "Don't open it here." I placed the envelope in my pocket. "There's a car parked behind the station. Wait until you're in it before you open the envelope. Then, head straight to that location."

Knowing that I would be with her calmed many of Harriet's concerns.

"The captain telephoned the owner and arranged to have some clean clothes brought to the hotel for both of you when you arrive," John assured her as if predicting what her next question would be, "However, I strongly suggest that you stay wherever he's sending you and not leave there until you're given instructions to do so."

He looked over at Harriet to emphasize his point. "That won't be a problem again, will it, Miss Doyel?"

The brunette shook her head. Her cheeks reddened with embarrassment at her recent mistake. I was sure that it was one she wouldn't make a second time.

"I'll keep an eye on her," I said, "She'll be fine with me."

John smirked, "I'm sure she will be."

At that moment, he noticed Dolores returning from the cleaners.

"Ah, Dolores, would you mind showing Miss Doyel to the car out back? I need to talk to Clive for a moment."

The secretary smiled warmly and nodded before escorting Harriet out of my office and down the hall.

Once they were out of sight, John sighed, exhausted, and rubbed his eyelids. Something was troubling him.

"What is it?" I asked.

John stroked his mouth nervously. "It's getting dangerous out there, Clive. I'm not a gambling man, but I'm willing to bet that Daugherty has heard about what happened at Harriet's apartment by now. He's probably got most of the Black Clovers searching this city for the two of you. You need to be careful. This place can't afford to lose another good cop."

Losing the rookie had shaken John.

"Daugherty has people everywhere. You can be damn sure that most of them will not be wearing a pin to help you identify them."

I assumed this much. Daugherty had already sent his clowns after us to try and force us into telling them where Lawrence's briefcase was. Because his brash attempts to find it had failed, it stood to reason he'd try a less direct approach the next time around.

"I know that, but I'm not Craig Lewis. I'm more than capable of taking care of myself," I reminded him, losing my patience, "Honestly, John, you make it sound like I've never done this before. I've been doing this for a while. I know the risks that come with the job. Or have you forgotten the first thing they teach you when you become a gumshoe: Assume that everyone's gunning for you until they give you a solid reason to think otherwise. I'm not some easy mark. I'll be fine."

John shook his head, "All I'm saying is, be careful. I've seen you and Miss Doyel making eyes at each other. You can't afford to get distracted. Remember, you're a detective first and a romantic second. If you're busy making goo-goo eyes at Miss Doyel, you're not paying attention to everyone else around you. That's when mistakes happen. You've got a job to do."

Having beaten his point to death, there was nothing more to say. Letting out another sigh, John headed toward the office door.

"Now, if you'll excuse me, I need to fill out some paperwork and inform the Lewis family that their son is dead," he said bitterly before exiting my office.

I also reached for the knob to leave but stopped in my tracks.

More than likely, John was right about Daugherty having people everywhere (among other things). Daugherty was connected with people high and low. What if one of those connections happened to be a dirty cop?

As much as I trusted many of the cops at the station, that didn't mean they were all impervious to corruption. Money has a way of getting people to do surprising things when enough of it's on the table. If Daugherty had bribed one into doing something illegal, like stealing evidence, what would stop them from taking Lawrence's briefcase and delivering it to the sick crime boss while I was out of the office?

The more I thought about it, the more it seemed unwise to leave the briefcase and the key together in my office. I quickly walked over to my desk, grabbed the brass key off it, and placed it into my pocket before heading out of my office and locking the door behind me.

A short time later, I met Harriet and Dolores near the station's back entrance. Both women stood in the doorway, waiting patiently for my arrival.

"There you are," Harriet said, "For a moment, I thought you weren't coming."

I smiled, "No. No. You won't get rid of me that easily."

Dolores opened the door. A car with a dark navy-blue finish was parked a few feet from it. It was rather dull looking, which was exactly what we needed to keep our heads down.

"Harriet, why don't you run ahead? I'll be half a moment."

The brunette hurried out to the car. When she was out of earshot, I turned to Dolores.

"I need you to do me a favor, Dee. During your lunch break tomorrow, I need you to head over to Marshall Fields and purchase a briefcase identical to Lawrence's for me." I subtly slipped a few large bills into the pocket of her coat.

"Once you have it, drop it off in my office. Make sure it's out of sight and keep the door locked as soon as you leave."

"Is that all?

I shook my head. "When Mason comes in, have him go into my office and grab the blueprints in my desk drawer. Tell him to keep them with the *essentials* until I'm back. He'll know what I mean. Then, have him return Lawrence's briefcase down to evidence and make sure it's locked up tight. Do you understand?"

The secretary nodded, though her concern was as clear as the glasses on her face. "But, what's going on?

"Nothing you need to worry about. Just being careful is all," I told her, "That being said, it's probably best that we keep this between us."

"Of course," she agreed.

As I turned to leave, she stopped me. "Where are the two of you going?"

"I'm afraid I can't tell you that." When the worry on her face lingered, I added, "Don't you fret. This'll be duck soup. I'm sure Harriet and I will be bored to death the entire time."

Dolores raised an unconvinced eyebrow and tittered at the apparent sarcasm in my last remark. She glanced over at Harriet.

"I'm sure..." she answered in kind. Without another word, she continued inside.

As soon as the door closed behind me, I followed Harriet and joined her in the car.

Against my better judgment (and the protests of my injured body), I climbed into the driver's seat. A moment later, I reached into my pocket and opened the envelope John had given me. After reading the piece of paper inside, I turned to Harriet.

"Do you have a light?"

She nodded and handed me her lighter.

To prevent the location from falling into the wrong hands, I quickly poked the corner of the paper into the tiny flame until it was nothing more than ash.

"Where are we going?" the doe-eyed woman asked.

With a smile, I placed the key in the ignition and started the engine. "I'll tell you on the way."

After driving for an hour, we pulled up to a sign for the Des Plaines Methodist Campground and continued onto the quiet thirty-five-acre property. There were still a few hours before dawn, so the campground was dark. As we drove past snow-covered trees, we encountered several boarded-up cottages along the way, many of which had fallen into disrepair. I wondered if I'd brought us to the right place.

Finally, I spotted a large wooden building up ahead. The building looked like it had seen better days (though it was not nearly as bad as many of the cottages we'd passed). The last few years have done a number on small businesses like this one. Between the war and the Stock Crash of 1929, it was a miracle this place hadn't closed down.

Inspecting the building, I counted at least fourteen windows around it. All of them were dark. I considered turning around until I noticed the sign above the porch: *Red Gables Hotel.*

"This is the place," I said reluctantly.

Harriet frowned, "You can't be serious. There's no one here! It's a dump!"

I chuckled to myself. Foster had been right; it was not the Ritz.

"Look at it this way, doll, this is the last place Daugherty would ever expect us to be hiding."

The sound logic didn't satisfy Harriet in the slightest.

"There's nobody here," she repeated.

The front door swung open at that moment, and a warmly dressed woman stepped onto the porch carrying a flashlight. Upon seeing our car, she gave a friendly wave.

"You were saying?" I teased. The unamused brunette responded by sending a very cross look my way.

I parked the car and led Harriet across the snowy pathway until we reached the porch. The other woman quickly ushered us through the door.

"Please come inside, before you catch your death of cold."

Harriet and I were far too cold to argue with the woman and hurried inside.

The woman switched on the light once we were out of the cold weather. No longer in the dark, we found ourselves in what appeared to be a small lobby that desperately needed cleaning and repairs. Large sheets covered nearby tables and chairs caked with dust and a sprinkling of cobwebs. Even the dirty rug could have used a good beating and washing. Much to my relief, none of the windows appeared broken, so the bitter cold remained outside. I spotted a wooden check-in counter with a large hotel mailbox behind it and a flight of stairs that needed more than a few new coats of fresh paint.

The woman retreated behind the dusty counter in front of the hotel mailbox.

"You'll have to excuse the mess," the woman apologized, "I'm afraid you caught us during our off-season. We were hoping to begin our renovations in the spring. The hotel usually isn't open this time of year, but we're willing to make a special exception in your case."

She looked down at a notebook.

"You must be the ones that the policeman called about earlier. Someone named, Captain Shoemaker, if I remember correctly?"

I nodded, "Yes. That's us."

"Splendid! I'm Mrs. Hattie Boone, the hostess of this hotel. I've seen to it that two of our nicest rooms have been made available to you. Here at the Red Gables Hotel, we aim to make sure your stay is a comfortable one."

"How kind of you," I said politely.

"Let me assure you; your stay here will be completely off the record."

That was a relief. "Unfortunately, because our entire staff is off for the season, the two of you will have the entire hotel to yourselves," Mrs. Boone said, "but you both are more than welcome to whatever food you find in the kitchen, should you get hungry."

Harriet seemed to like the idea of staying here less and less.

"Thank you. We will keep that in mind," I said, ignoring the bitter expression on Harriet's face.

The hostess handed us a pair of hotel room keys.

"Before you arrived, I made sure that some fresh clothes were brought up to each of your rooms from what was left in the chapel's donation closet. I do hope they fit you."

"That was very generous of you. Thank you again."

"Would you like me to show you up to your rooms?" the hostess asked.

I shook my head, "No thanks. I think the two of us can manage."

"Very well. I will let you get settled in then," she said politely, "I'll be back in two days to see how you are doing. Please enjoy your stay."

Harriet and I continued up the stairs and into our hotel rooms. Neither of us had brought luggage, so there was nothing to unpack. As it happened, our rooms were directly across each other, making it easier to keep an eye on her.

The room was what you would usually expect from a hotel room: A comfy bed. A nice dresser. Somewhat clean curtains (though some dust had collected in the fabric). A tall lamp for added light. A small washroom with a bathtub, sink, and toilet was connected to the room. Based on the state of the rest of the hotel, I can only guess what the plumbing situation was, but I was in no rush to find out either.

I carefully surveyed the small room, checking the closet and washroom for unwanted visitors. Thankfully, I found none.

Upon opening the dresser drawer, I found pairs of clean clothes, just as the hostess had said. Judging by the wear on the fabric, it became clear that the clothes had passed through several hands over the years and would likely be retired soon after I was through using them during my stay. With any luck, we wouldn't be here long enough to go through my entire wardrobe.

A short time later, I knocked on the door to Harriet's room.

"Who is it?"

I was a little surprised at the question, considering we were the only occupants in the hotel. "It's Clive," I answered.

The lovely brunette answered the door wearing clean casual clothes that looked much newer than I'd received. Harriet wore a burgundy dress with four matching buttons on the abdomen and a trim waist belt made from the same fabric as the dress. It was much more modest than what she usually wore, but the look suited her, nonetheless.

"Mind if I come in?" I asked, standing in the doorway.

"Of course," she said warmly, "Is everything all right?"

I nodded, "Everything's fine. No one followed us. We'll be safe here for a few days, as long as we keep our heads down."

Harriet laughed playfully, "I'm sure it'll be much easier to stay put, now that you're here with me."

Like my room, her room had all the same furniture as mine, though Mrs. Boone had taken the time to do a much more thorough job dusting than she had mine. There was not a cobweb in sight.

The blood-covered dress Harriet had been wearing before had been discarded in the waste basket beside the bed. Her mood had drastically improved (I'm sure the change of clothes had a hand in it).

In the short time we'd arrived in our rooms, Harriet had wasted no time laying out her "new" clothes across the comforter to help her decide which she wanted to wear first. All the choices would look exceptionally beautiful on her. I also noted that the brunette had been given a much more comprehensive clothing selection than mine.

"I see you've been making yourself at home."

Harriet's cheeks flushed. She quickly gathered the clothes on the bed into a large bundle in her arms and tossed them onto the closet floor.

"Oh yes," she blushed, "I was having trouble deciding what to wear. So I figured I'd take a look at all my options."

"I see."

"Won't you sit down?" she added, patting the edge of the bed.

"Well, if you insist."

Once I'd sat down, Harriet joined me on the bed.

She let out a yawn. Despite her attempts to convince herself and me that she wasn't tired, the heavy bags under her eyes suggested otherwise.

"You look tired. I can leave and let you rest for a while if you like," I suggested.

"Me? I'm not tired." She yawned again. "Whatever gave you that idea?"

I couldn't help but smile. "You make a compelling argument." Her eyelids started to droop. "Honestly, Harriet, when was the last time you slept?"

The nodding brunette shook herself awake. Realizing she couldn't keep the lie up, she sighed. "The night my club went up in flames. The night you stayed at my apartment and kept watch. I-I haven't been able to sleep on my own. I don't know what it is ... but having you near me makes me feel safe."

She was struggling to keep her eyes open. I gently brushed her hair aside. The poor girl was exhausted.

"If I promise to stay until you fall asleep, will you get some rest?" I whispered. Harriet gave a tired nod. "Then, lay back and rest your head. I'll be here when you wake up."

The sleepy woman crawled over to the pillows, softly placed her head on them, and closed her eyes. I ran my fingers through her hair and lightly caressed her scalp.

Harriet smiled at the sensation. "Oh, that feels nice..." she cooed, "...Aren't you tired?"

"Not in the slightest," I yawned, but Harriet didn't hear me. She was already fast asleep.

I couldn't blame her. It had been a long and tiring day for both of us. *Maybe sleep was the best medicine for the occasion*, I thought while stroking her hair.

The sound of the sleeping woman's breathing assured me that her slumber was peaceful. It was music to my ears.

A moment later, I drifted off to sleep as well.

CHAPTER 16

An Angel in My Arms

Harriet and I woke up in each other's arms, feeling well-rested and in much better spirits. I was the first to wake up. My eyes drifted over to the sleeping beauty in my arms.

Harriet was sound asleep. Her dainty hand rested softly against my chest, her long, slender body curled up around my arm. Locks of her chestnut hair cascaded over her pillow. The daylight peeked through the window and hit her body, making her glow like the angel she was. I doubted even the most gifted artists could have captured the serene beauty of that moment.

I was afraid to move, afraid to breathe, in fear that I might wake her.

The more I gazed at her sleeping form, the more I realized how different she was from every dame that came before. She was far brighter than some of the girls that had come and gone in my life–many of whom had more air than brains lurking under the curls on their heads. Harriet knew what she wanted in life and seized every opportunity that came her way. Despite having fame and power, she was still concerned about the people around her. She had a gentle nature about her that she rarely let the world see.

Apart from her brains and wit, she also had beauty–an uncommon combination. Even fast asleep, she was mesmerizing. How her chest rose and fell with every soft breath she took was enough to make any man's heart skip a beat. Unlike many of the dames I'd spent my lonely nights with, I wanted Harriet to stick around when all this was over.

I was head over heels for her. At that moment, I knew without a shadow of a doubt that I would do anything to keep her safe.

Harriet stirred slightly; then her eyes fluttered open. She smiled as soon as she saw my face.

"Good morning," she sighed.

"Good morning," I said, "You look like you slept well."

"I did."

"Glad to hear it."

"How about you?" she asked, "How did you sleep?"

"Well enough," I shrugged, "though, your snoring kept me awake."

Her mouth dropped open playfully. "I don't snore!"

"Yes, you do," I teased, "as loud as a train."

She gave my arm a light slap and giggled. "You take that back, mister! I'll have you know, I'm a refined lady."

"Are you now?" I chuckled. Harriet raised her hand to slap me again, but I held up my hands in surrender. "I'm only joking."

After kissing my good cheek quickly, she rolled onto her back. "Oh, I could get used to waking up like this every morning..."

"Well, considering we have the entire hotel to ourselves, I don't think that'll be a problem."

"No. I mean, having you here with me when I wake up," she explained, "I feel safe having you around. It's like having my own personal guardian angel."

"I'm not much of an angel," I admitted.

Harriet rolled over and looked me in the eyes. She placed a gentle hand on my cheek.

"You are to me. I know you're a good man. Do you have any idea how difficult it is to find a decent man in this city?

"I've been around enough creeps to know the good ones from the bad. You are one of the good ones, Clive Hill."

"Creeps?" I joked.

The brunette slapped my arm again. "No, silly. Men." I only shook my head and smiled. "I'm being serious. You are the first man in my life who hasn't tried to take advantage of me to get something." She blushed. "If I'm being honest, every time you're near me, most of me wants to pin you down and plant one on you until my lips get sore."

"Then, why don't you?"

Harriet's eyes filled with excitement. I imagine part of her was wondering whether or not she was still dreaming. Whatever she was thinking didn't stop her from leaning forward and planting her luscious lips against mine. Her lips tasted as sweet as honey.

As our kiss became more passionate, I wrapped my arm around her back and pulled her closer to me to deepen the kiss.

A moment later, she broke it with a small gasp to catch her breath. I could feel her heart racing. Her smile widened.

"That was better than the one you gave me last night!" she giggled, "You sure know how to take a girl's breath away."

"Years of practice," I admitted before resuming our necking for a few more minutes.

Eventually, we had to take a short break. Both Harriet and I panted loudly as we attempted to steady our breath. Our clothes had long since been tossed off the bed and rested on the floor in several small, disorganized clumps. As we lay there staring at each other, Harriet took my hand.

"Clive..."

"Yes?"

"I can't begin to thank you for everything you've done for me. You've pulled me back from a very dark place on more than one occasion these past couple of days." There were tears in her eyes. "If you hadn't been there to help me ... I-I don't know where I'd be."

She wiped the tears from her eyes, then looked away bashfully and tried to hide her face in her hands.

"I don't usually say this ... and I'm not entirely sure where to begin. So, please bear with me ..."

Harriet took a deep breath, collected her thoughts, and uncovered her face.

"Everything you told me last night, about being better than Daugherty, made me realize that you see the real me. I don't need to put on a brave face or pretend to be someone I'm not when I'm with you. So here I am. No more hiding. No more masks. I want to be completely honest with you. So, I'm just going to say it ... I think I'm in love with you, Clive Hill."

A small chuckle escaped my mouth. Harriet eyed me, not sure what to make of my reaction.

"What's so funny?"

I reached out and gently caressed her cheek with my thumb. "I was just thinking the same thing."

The lovestruck woman launched her body at me and began kissing my face. Her sudden and eager movement resulted in a pained groan from me as her body bumped against my bruised torso.

"Take it easy there, toots," I grunted, "I was lucky to survive a beating from Daugherty's goons last night. I don't know if I'll be able to survive you if you come at me like that again."

Harriet blushed. "I'm sorry."

"It's all right," I laughed once the pain subsided. "Just try and be a little more careful the next time you decide to pounce on me."

"I'll keep that in mind," she said, giving a gentler kiss this time before we picked up where we left off.

An hour or so later, we made our way downstairs and headed to the dining hall building. Because it was the offseason, Harriet and I had the whole hall to ourselves. Unfortunately, that also meant there was no staff in the kitchen to prepare anything for us.

Being the culinary genius I am, I rummaged through the pantry and prepared an exquisite lunch for the two of us—a pair of onion and ketchup sandwiches on slightly stale bread. *Who says chivalry is dead?*

We spent the rest of the day trying to entertain ourselves in every way possible. Harriet was excellent company to have during the otherwise uneventful day. I was beginning to understand how being cooped up in an apartment alone all day made Harriet feel the need to escape it. Had she not been with me, I would've taken my chances back in the city.

Later in the afternoon, the two of us strolled around the grounds. It was chilly, but getting out of the hotel was excellent. The blanket of virgin snow around us covered everything from the tops of the trees to the ground below. All in all, it was a beautiful sight.

To our right was the Des Plaines River—a thin layer of ice gathered by the water's edge. The heavy snow caused the surrounding branches to hang over the running water in a slight arch. The sound of the running water had a calming effect—something the two of us took a moment to appreciate. When the summer months came, I was confident all the snow was bound to cause flooding once it melted, but right now, it was lovely.

As the sun began to set, we returned to the hotel. Not long after, we climbed into bed and retired for the night.

CHAPTER 17

A Case Gone Frosty

On Monday morning, as Harriet and I passed through the lobby on our way out to the dining hall for brunch, we were surprised when the hotel telephone rang. It had not gone off all week, so hearing the loud ringing after days of silence was strange. I stopped beside it.

Harriet looked at me, confused.

I waved her on, "You go ahead. I'll meet you outside."

She shrugged and continued out the door.

As the telephone rang, I lifted the handset and placed it to my ear.

"Hello, this is the Red Gables Hotel. How can we help you?" I said, trying to sound like the concierge of the small hotel. The voice that answered was one I recognized immediately.

"Hill, it's Captain Shoemaker. I have a lot to do, so I'll cut to the chase ... Cyrus Daugherty is dead."

I could hardly believe my ears.

"Dead, sir?"

"Is there an echo over there? Yes, dead."

A wave of relief washed over me. "That's... good news. If you don't mind me asking, how did it happen?"

"According to the morning paper, he died sometime last night. 'Sounds like his illness finally caught up with him."

Judging by the way he'd been coughing the night I'd visited him, that seemed the most likely cause of death. If I'm being honest, part of me was disappointed that the Irish bastard had kicked the bucket before he was able to answer for his crimes. The people who'd been killed as a result of the man's selfish ambitions deserved far more justice than Daugherty escaping judgment on account of his death. The very thought angered me—though I did not let it show.

"What happens now?" I asked, "Who's going to be held responsible for his crimes? What about Craig Lewis or Midnight Lawrence? Are we supposed to ignore the fact that Daugherty had a hand in their murders?"

There was a seriousness in the captain's tone. "What happened to Officer Lewis was a tragedy. No one denies that. Unfortunately, there isn't enough evidence that ties Daugherty to the Lawrence murder. Either way, we can't arrest a dead man.

"I'm sorry, but without any other suspects, the case will be thrown out." The regret in his voice was genuine—an emotion the hardened captain rarely let show. "Since there is no longer a threat to either you or Miss Doyel, the two of you can come out of hiding now. I expect to see you back in the office later."

When the call ended, I joined Harriet on the porch. She smiled.

"Was that the station?"

"It was," I reflected as I stood beside her.

"And—What did they want?"

I was still lost in my thoughts while processing the news.

Harriet noticed my distraction.

"Clive? Did you hear me?"

"Oh," I said, coming out of my daze, "I'm sorry. Yes. I heard you."

"Well ... What did they say?" she asked again.

"Cyrus Daugherty is dead..."

Her eyes widened. "Dead? How? When?"

"Sometime last night. They say the cause of death was consumption," I explained, "Probably died coughing up blood."

The young woman looked away.

"Sounds dreadful," she said, placing a hand at her throat, "I can't imagine dying from something like that..." Another thought crossed her mind. "What does that mean? Are we safe? Can we finally go home?"

"I guess so," I admitted.

"What happens now..." she asked, "... with the case, I mean..."

I took a deep breath, "The case will be thrown out. You can't exactly arrest someone for their crimes postmortem. The Justice System will consider Daugherty's death sufficient payment for his debt to society."

Harriet spun around angrily. The fire in her eyes burned so brightly that I was surprised it didn't melt the snow around us.

"That's it? That's all?" she shouted. "All his crimes disappear just like that? He burned down my club, murdered countless people, and tried to kidnap me! After all that, you're telling me the bastard gets off easy?"

"I'm afraid so."

"How is that justice?" Harriet huffed, "My building is gone! My apartment is a crime scene! It'll take months before they get all the repairs to it done! Who's going to pay for that?"

Tears of fury began to stream down her cheeks.

"What about Lawrence's briefcase? What happens to that? I deserve to have the ledgers in it! I should be able to use all the money that bastard owes me for burning down my business!"

"That's evidence," I explained, "The plans, the ledgers, even the money in Daugherty's account. We don't just turn that over."

Harriet continued to weep.

"But ... He owes me ..." she sniffled, "If Lawrence hadn't been killed, it would've been mine anyway ... It's not fair."

The poor woman had lost so much because of Cyrus Daugherty. I could understand why someone in Harriet's position would feel that they were owed some degree of compensation after the traumatic misfortune they'd been through. Unfortunately, I couldn't give her what she was asking for.

"I'm sorry, Harriet. I can't do that," I said gently, placing my hand on her shoulder, "But, for the time being, you're welcome to stay with me until the repairs to your apartment are finished."

Slowly, the brunette began to calm down.

After gathering our belongings and leaving our hotel keys in the lobby, we got in the car and drove back into the city. To my amazement, the morning traffic was better than I'd anticipated. For the most part, it was smooth sailing. Harriet and I reached the Police Headquarters building just before one o'clock.

John Foster was waiting for us near the lobby when we arrived. Before saying a word, I handed him the hanger with the clothes he'd let me borrow. Foster took a moment to inspect the clothes.

"Hmmm... Not a drop of blood on them," he laughed, "Must've been an uneventful couple of days."

"I wouldn't say that," Harriet giggled, momentarily taking my hand. "Uh-huh..." Foster agreed, noting the handholding but saying nothing on the matter.

Wrestling my hand from Harriet's grip, I stepped toward John and asked, "What can you tell me about Daugherty's death?"

John shifted uncomfortably, "That's a conversation best had in your office."

He and Harriet followed me down the hall and past Dolores's desk as I retrieved the keys from my pocket and unlocked the door to my office. Switching on the lights, I was relieved that everything was as I had left it. I traveled around the desk and gestured for John and Harriet to sit down. Once everyone was comfortable, I glanced over at John.

"What happened with Daugherty?" I asked, "I need facts, not gossip from the funny pages."

The other detective sighed, "According to the official report, one of the guards watching Daugherty last night said things had been very quiet. Then, without warning, Daugherty started coughing violently. Despite the guard's attempts to sit him up, Daugherty started coughing up blood until he finally stopped breathing altogether."

"Good," Harriet chimed in spitefully, "The bastard deserved to go out choking on his own blood!"

I ignored her. "Was there anything that suggested he might have been poisoned?"

"No," John said, shaking his head. "It was definitely the sickness that got him."

"What about Malone? Has anyone seen or heard from him in the past few days?"

Foster shook his head again, "Not to my knowledge. As far as I can tell, he's given this city the breeze."

Considering that Malone was the next in line to inherit Daugherty's empire, which included the Black Clovers, that seemed highly unlikely. A man with that much to gain would not just pack up and leave the throne unattended. If anything, he was probably lying low somewhere until things cooled down.

"Malone was Daugherty's righthand man," I pointed out, "I doubt he would skip town before he got his hands on the golden goose Daugherty was leaving him. Now that his boss is dead, he's in charge of the Black Clovers. He's not the kind of man to pass up an opportunity like that."

"We'll cross that bridge, if and when, he ever shows up again." He placed his hands behind his head and leaned back in the chair. "For now, just be content with the fact that another dangerous mobster has gone the way of the doo-doo."

"What about what happened to Midnight Lawrence? Are we going to just let whoever killed him roam free?" I argued.

John sighed and pinched the bridge of his nose. "We've had no leads for a couple of days. I think it's time you faced the facts. This case has gone so cold that it's practically frozen. You're just too stubborn to admit it."

Over my entire career, I prided myself on never leaving a case unfinished. Maybe John was right. We weren't even close to finding Lawrence's killer. As much as I hated to admit it, the odds of finding the killer were not in my favor.

"Tell you what," John said, sitting upright, "Why don't you take the rest of the day off? I'll cover your shift for you. You've been through a lot. Go out. Get some fresh air. Clear your head today."

The offer was enticing. I was seriously considering it. Only one thing was preventing it from happening. "I don't think the captain would like the idea of me taking off after I've been gone for a few days."

John waved his hand dismissively. "Don't you worry about the captain..." I wasn't entirely convinced. As if sensing my apprehension, he added, "Look. If it'll make you feel better, I'll pop into his office right now and talk to him about it."

"Are you mad?" I objected, but John was already on his feet and heading toward the door. Before I could argue, he slipped out of the office, leaving Harriet and me alone.

Harriet seemed excited by the idea. "Wouldn't that be nice? We could go to the zoo together. It'll be fun!"

Her foot knocked over the leather attaché case beside my desk as she stirred in her seat. She quickly lifted it off the floor and inspected it.

"What's this?"

"Lawrence's briefcase."

The excitement in her eyes intensified. "You mean, this is what Lawrence was going to sell me the other night?"

"I'm sure he would've kept the briefcase and let you keep what's inside—but yes. This is the case he had on him the night he was murdered," I admitted.

The eager brunette tried to open the ends of the locked briefcase. "That means Daugherty's ledgers and casino plans are inside!" She tugged harder. "I just want to take a quick peek..." She continued to struggle. "Come on! Open, damn it!" When it remained closed, she threw it on the floor in frustration.

"Hey! Careful with that!" I protested. "That's still evidence!"

"You have no idea how much I need this. Just one of those books could solve my problems! I could even use the blueprints to rebuild my club! I just need to see what's inside!"

I bent down and picked the briefcase off the floor. "I'm sorry, doll. I can't let you do that." I placed it behind my desk. "The only way you're getting in it is with this key..." I said, briefly showing her the small brass key in my pocket before placing it back. "Unfortunately, that's against the rules. It would violate several protocols. You understand."

Harriet let out a long-disappointed sigh, "I guess..."

I looked her way sympathetically. "Believe me, I wish I could, but my hands are tied."

"I understand..."

"I wouldn't worry about making ends meet," I assured her, "You're a talented woman. You'll find work in no time."

Harriet glanced over at me and smiled. "Well, if I can't have the money, at least I'm not walking away from this whole ordeal empty-handed. I did get to spend plenty of time with you, handsome. That wasn't so bad."

"Play your cards right and I'm sure we'll see a lot more of each other."

Her widening smile and pleasant laughter made it impossible to keep from smiling myself. I was dizzy with the dame. Harriet had a point; even though the case had gone cold, it had brought us together. I'd say that was worth the trouble.

Just then, John knocked on the office door. He stepped in with a victorious smile. "It's done. The captain agreed to give you the rest of the day off," he said proudly.

"How'd you manage that?" I laughed, rather impressed he'd pulled off the feat so quickly.

John put his palm to his heart. "You doubted me? Ouch. You know, you're not the only one who knows how to turn on the charm." When I chuckled again, he added, "I can be charming when I want to be. I only mentioned how disappointed you were about having to close the Lawrence case like that. After all, you've never left a case unfinished. I told him it was a matter of pride. And just like that, Captain Shoemaker agreed to let you have the rest of the day off. Of course, you'll need to work tomorrow, but I'm sure that you're fine with that."

I nodded. It was a fair trade. At least having some extra time with Harriet would help keep my mind off my failure to get Daugherty's victims the justice they deserved. But I suppose that was just the nature of the beast.

"Thank you," I said, unable to find the exact words to express my gratitude.

John just chuckled, "We'll just say you owe me one. Now, what are you still hanging around here for? You're burning daylight. Go out and enjoy your day off."

CHAPTER 18

A Brief Getaway

Harriet and I took a cab to the Lincoln Park Zoo that afternoon. Despite the snow and brisk weather–which was only made colder by the breeze created by Lake Michigan–we were surprised to see the zoo as crowded as it was. Little youngsters dressed in their winter coats, wool hats, scarves, boots, and knitted mittens wandered around the zoo accompanied by their parents, grandparents, and nannies. At the same time, groups of older children eagerly ran to see all the attractions.

Although one or two enclosures had been closed, most of the exhibits remained open year-round. As strange as it may seem, many of the animals had grown accustomed to the cold weather and continued their day as usual.

As we walked, we spotted several families of bears, including polar bears, brown bears, and even a few black bears. A family of penguins seemed right at home in the chilly weather and happily shuffled around in their dapper suits of black and white. Some even plunged headfirst into the waters of their artificial habitat. There were Giraffes with long necks that towered over the crowds, a bob of seals swimming around in a pool, and a few other animals near the Lion House.

Eventually, Harriet grabbed me by the hand and led me to the Primate House. We hurried inside and saw a few of the smaller ape exhibits before arriving at the section of the building where a large group had gathered to see Bushman the Gorilla.

The six-foot, 550-pound gorilla sat in his cage and entertained the crowds with his sheer size. Being the first gorilla to live in Chicago, Bushman quickly became a beloved resident of the zoo. Since his arrival four years ago, his fame made him the face of the Lincoln Park Zoo.

"Isn't he something?" Harriet asked, her face beaming with excitement.

"He is," I agreed, "Think he wants a job at the station?"

She giggled, "What a sight that would be!"

"He'd sure make criminals think twice before breaking the law."

Once Harriet had finished admiring Bushman, we headed toward the exit. The brunette did a little twirl in place and spun into my arms.

"Oh, Clive, I'm having such a wonderful time," she sighed, "Thank you for taking me here."

I smiled. "Glad to see you're enjoying yourself."

She looked up at me, her brown eyes twinkled with adoration. As I stared at her, I felt myself sinking deeper and deeper in love with her, like I was wearing a pair of cement galoshes in the lake. Unable to contain herself any longer,

Harriet wrapped her arms around my waist and pressed her lips against mine. I closed my eyes and enjoyed the sensation. She caressed down my back using her left hand while her right was placed on my hip.

A family of four passed by us on their way out, visibly uncomfortable with our display of affection. The mother shielded her children's eyes and quickly ushered them through the exit.

Harriet blushed, "I'm sorry. I got a tad bit caught up in the moment."

"What'd you say we get out of this doorway and see some of the other animals?" I suggested.

Shortly after returning outside, we visited enclosures that housed zebra, takin, camels, exotic kangaroos shipped over from Australia, deer, and antelope. In one of the enclosures, we spotted a moose whose antlers were so large that it was a miracle it could lift its head at all.

An icy breeze ran down Harriet's back, causing her to shiver suddenly.

"Brrr..." she said, pulling her coat tighter around herself.

"Is it just me, or does it feel like it's getting colder?"

"It is a bit nippy," I admitted, "I was considering grabbing a nice warm cup of joe for myself..." I wasn't really, but I didn't want the poor shivering girl to freeze. "I could grab you something while I'm there."

The two of us made our way to the lagoon and approached the two-story red brick building with a green roof covered by snow. Even from a distance, I could read the gold-painted letters above the large serving window: *Café Brauer.*

I paused near the frozen lagoon in front of the building and turned to Harriet once again.

"Last chance, doll. Did you want something? I'm buying."

The brunette fastened her coat tighter to keep warm and nodded.

"C-C-Coco," she said through chattering teeth. "P-Please..."

"One hot coco, coming right up," I said, "Wait here. I'll be back in a moment."

Leaving the shivering woman where she was, I continued on a couple more feet until I reached the service window.

A waiter appeared. "What can I get you?"

"One cup of joe and a hot coco."

"Anything else?"

I shook my head, "No. Just that."

The waiter nodded and began working on the order. A moment later, he frowned. "It'll be a minute or two. I gotta grab another can of coco powder from the back..."

"That's fine," I said as the man disappeared in the back.

While I waited, I turned around and glanced back at Harriet. *Right where I left you*, I thought to myself. I crossed my arms and leaned against the counter. It was then that I realized she wasn't alone. Standing beside her was none other than Lenny Riggs.

They were discussing something, but I was too far to hear it. Whatever the bag of bones was telling her had Harriet visibly confused.

In a flash, I heard the screech of tires, and a black car raced down the street and pulled up next to the south gate. Before I knew what was happening, Riggs grabbed the startled woman, tossed her over his shoulder with far more strength than a man his size should have been able to, and sprinted toward the car.

Harriet screamed and attempted to resist her kidnapper, but her efforts did little to slow him down.

Wasting no time, I ran to cut them off before they reached the street. Unfortunately, Riggs was also much faster than he appeared.

As I turned the corner of the building, I saw Riggs toss the screaming brunette into the car's trunk and forcefully shut it.

The skinny man booked it to the vehicle's passenger side and climbed in.

From the inside of the car, I heard a familiar voice.

"Drive! Drive!" Mal Malone shouted to the driver.

I watched in horror as the tires screeched against the pavement. I could hear Harriet's muffled screams from the trunk as the black car sped away. There was nothing I could do but watch as the car quickly disappeared from view.

The effort I'd exerted during my pursuit left me very winded. My bruised lungs–which were still recovering–burned while I attempted to catch my breath. I placed my hands on my hips. Something felt off.

Patting my pockets, I soon realized the brass key to Lawrence's briefcase was missing. Only one person had been close enough to take it from me–someone who'd known exactly where I'd been keeping it.

"Harriet..." She and the key were now in the hands of Malone and the Black Clovers.

CHAPTER 19

Call From a Clover

After returning to Central Headquarters, I sat in my office with John, Mason Wayne, and Jim Douglas. I lit a cigarette and puffed it silently while I reviewed what had happened for the hundredth time in my head. Some of the facts were clear: *Malone had snatched Harriet in broad daylight. Harriet had the key to Lawrence's briefcase. One of Harriet's loyal admirers was working for Mal Malone.*

Others, I needed to piece together: *How had Malone known where to find us? How had I missed the Lenny Riggs angle? Where was Harriet now?* And most importantly, *who killed Midnight Lawrence?*

My only logical conclusion was that Malone had someone watching the police station for him. When they saw Harriet and I leave, they likely followed us to the zoo and then tipped their boss off to our location.

It made sense that the new head of the Black Clovers had sent Lenny Riggs to approach Harriet the way he did. A familiar face like his wouldn't raise an alarm like a squad of thugs. When Harriet lowered her guard, Riggs moved in when she was alone and snatched her before she could get away. It almost would've been impressive—if it hadn't been illegal.

Unfortunately, I wasn't able to answer the other questions just yet.

John hung his head, "Clive ... I'm sorry. If I'd known Malone was still watching you—"

"It's fine..." I finally said, "You couldn't have known."

We sat in uncomfortable silence for another moment until Jim Douglas asked:

"Any idea where Malone might've taken Miss Doyel?"

I shook my head, "She could be anywhere."

"Has he made a list of demands?" Mason chimed in, "Or tried to contact you yet?"

"Not yet..."

The telephone on Dolores's desk rang in the other room.

"...but I'm sure, it'll only be a matter of time before he does."

A minute later, she knocked on the door.

"Come in."

The secretary poked her head into the office. She looked nervous.

"Um, Clive ... There's a man on the line that wants to talk to you. H-He says you'll want to take his call..."

Malone, I guessed. I'd expected something like this.

"Thank you, Dolores," I told her, "Send it through."

The telephone in my office rang a moment later. I held a finger to my lips, gesturing for John and the others to remain silent as I picked up the handset.

"This is Hill."

The voice on the other end sounded cocky.

"Detective," Malone said, "Glad I caught you in the office. I trust you enjoyed your time at the zoo."

I shrugged. "Eh–There were too many apes running around for my liking. It's more enjoyable when the apes stay in their cages."

"Not all of them like being in cages." He was well aware that we weren't talking about animals.

I didn't have time for idle chit-chat. The bastard had Harriet.

"I don't have all day. Why don't you cut the malarkey and tell me what you want?"

"You know exactly what I want. Lawrence's briefcase. The one with the ledgers and blueprints he swiped from Mr. Daugherty." His tone was focused, with a slightly threatening quality to it. "And before you start playin' dumb, we already found the key to it on the dame when we searched her. Thoroughly."

My hand balled into a fist. I felt my jaw tighten. The thought of some lowlife putting his grubby mitts all over Harriet made my blood boil.

Malone continued, "We know you have the briefcase. If you didn't, we wouldn't be having this conversation. So, if you don't want us to start shipping the girl back to you piece by piece, you're gonna listen good."

"I'm all ears," I said begrudgingly.

"At midnight, you're going to bring the briefcase and everything in it, over to the Grant Statue in Lincoln Park. I'll be waiting in the tunnel under it. Come alone. If you're late, the girl dies. If you try and double-cross me, she dies.

'You don't bring the goods I asked for, she dies. 'You try any funny business during the exchange, she dies. 'I get the feeling anything is off—"

"She dies," I interrupted, "Yes. You've made that clear. While all of that's just fine and dandy, how do I know you haven't killed her already?"

The voice on the line chuckled, "You're in no position to start making demands. But, since you seem so concerned..."

In the background, I heard a door swing open. Somewhere in the distance, I could make out what sounded like muffled protests and someone struggling. I could only assume one of the goons was trying to remove the gag from the struggling person.

Harriet's terrified screams filled the silence a moment later.

"Clive! Clive!"

Malone's voice returned, "All right, that's enough. Get her outta here."

The goons must've placed the gag back over her mouth because her screams died down again, and the sounds of struggling became more and more distant.

"Satisfied?" he asked, not expecting an answer, "Good. I'll be waiting..."

The line went dead.

Slowly, I hung the phone back on the hook.

"What did he want?" Foster finally asked after a brief moment of silence."

“He wants to trade Harriet for Lawrence's briefcase," I told him, "I'm supposed to bring it with me to the Grant Statue at midnight for the exchange. If I don't, they'll kill her."

John looked at me like I was out of my gourd. "You're not seriously considering this, are you?" When I remained silent, he said, "You realize you're walking into a trap."

I nodded, "Oh, I'm well aware of that. But he has Harriet. I'm not going into this half-cocked."

John blinked, "Listen to yourself. In the unlikely event that they don't kill you and take the briefcase the moment you show up, you'll be a sitting duck!"

"Not to mention, you'll be handing evidence over to a known gangster," Douglas added, "Last time I checked, that was illegal. If, by some miracle, you get out of this alive, Captain Shoemaker will have your badge!"

A smile crept across my face. "I've no intention of breaking the law or losing my badge."

I held up the briefcase behind my desk.

"Before Harriet and I went into hiding, I had Dolores purchase a briefcase identical to the one Lawrence had on him the night he was murdered." I looked over at Mason. "Do you still have the *essentials* I asked you to look at in your office?"

Mason nodded.

"While Lawrence's actual briefcase is still locked up in evidence, its contents were exchanged for dummy ledgers," I revealed, "I left the real ones with Mason for safekeeping, in case someone tried to break into the evidence locker."

The new information didn't sit well with John.

"So, let me get this straight, in addition to taking actual evidence—"

"Relocating evidence," I corrected, "Technically, the real evidence never left the building."

John frowned, "You replaced actual evidence with decoys and passed them off as the real thing..." Realization flashed across his face. "Oh, no ... No. No. No. I know that look. Bad idea. Once Malone realizes you've pulled the old switcheroo with the dummy ledgers, he's going to kill you."

He had a point, but as he had previously stated, Malone was probably thinking of doing that anyway. To avoid an early grave, I needed to stay one step ahead of the newly promoted gangster.

"I've already taken that into consideration..."

I spent the remainder of the hour going over my plan.

Once we concluded our meeting, Foster and the others cleared out of my office and left me to prepare for the exchange with Malone. I spent the next few hours gathering all the materials I needed to put my plan into effect, then left the office a few minutes before eleven-thirty.

CHAPTER 20

Tricks of the Trade

Midnight was quickly approaching when I arrived at Lincoln Park. It was dark. The only light illuminating my path came from the park lights operating well after closing. The light it cast created ominous shadows in the darkness. Hundreds of footprints were in the snow from earlier that day, making it difficult to determine whether they were old or fresh. Either way, the hairs on my neck told me I wasn't alone.

As I continued down the path toward my destination, I opened my silver cigarette case and lit a cigarette to combat the chilly breeze that Lake Michigan created. Once my lungs were filled with the warm air, I placed the small metal case back inside the left inner pocket of my jacket and let the smoke pass my lips.

A few minutes later, I could see the bronze statue of Ulysses S. Grant and the rest of the granite monument below it. The Romanesque-style structure consisted of two levels below the eighteen-foot statue and the pillar it sat on. A terrace covered with a stone roof and five arched doorways made up the middle portion of the monument. The lower section had an enormous arch at its base that formed a small tunnel. Beside it was a pair of stone steps leading up to the terrace. It was the ideal place for Malone to set up an ambush.

I gripped the leather handles of Lawrence's attaché case tighter as I approached. When I didn't see Malone, Harriet—or anyone else for that matter—I glanced down at my wristwatch. It was still a few minutes before midnight, so I was on time. The feeling that there were several eyes watching me from the shadows did not go away. Where was Malone?

"Malone ... I'm here, like you asked," I called into the darkness. No one answered. "I have the briefcase with me. Are we going to do this or what?"

A shadowy figure appeared at the end of the tunnel. Its footsteps echoed as it got closer, accompanied by a tapping noise every second step. A moment later, Mal Malone stepped into the light.

Malone was dressed in a thick black winter coat that stopped at his knees. He wore a grey wool scarf that concealed the lapel pin.

Snowflakes stuck to the fabric of the snap-brim hat that covered his head. Unlike the last time I'd seen him, the mobster walked with a cane and a noticeable limp on his right side. Each step he took was stiff and visibly pained—which tends to happen when you've had a knife buried deep into the meat of your thigh.

"Detective..." Malone said, leaning against his cane, "... You're early. Nice of you to show."

"Where's Harriet?" I asked. There was no time for pleasantries. I was there for one purpose. "I held up my end of the deal. Now, where is she?"

"She's here," the gangster said cryptically, "Why don't you hand over the case and I'll have someone bring her out?"

"I'm not giving you anything until I see her first," I countered. "I'll only make the trade when she's present, not before."

"Very well," Malone sighed, clearly annoyed that I was making demands of my own, "Riggs, bring the girl down here."

The bony weasel appeared at the top of the staircase to my left, with a gagged woman beside him. Harriet's hands were bound with a thick rope, with a similar rope held at her neck. Her frightened eyes went wide with panic as she started to struggle. The gag in her mouth muffled the brunette's protests. Riggs tugged the rope at her throat forcefully while they descended the stone steps and took their place beside Malone.

"See, detective, she's perfectly fine. I'm a man of my word. Now, toss over the briefcase."

I shook my head, "Not until Harriet goes free!"

"You're in no position to be making demands, detective."

Riggs pulled the rope across Harriet's throat tighter, cutting off her airway. The captive woman struggled for air; veins in her neck bulged while her bound hands desperately scrambled to slip her fingers under the rope, to no avail. Her gasps became more and more labored as the man tightened the rope.

"Stop!" I shouted, raising my hand above my head, "Here! Take it!"

I quickly tossed Lawrence's briefcase over to Malone. It landed with a *thud* at the mobster's feet.

Malone cocked his head and nodded to Riggs, who immediately let one side of the rope drop and gave the brunette a harsh shove in my direction.

Her unsteady footing caused her to fall to her knees, coughing and gasping for breath. I rushed over and helped her off the icy ground. When Harriet was in my arms, I removed the gag from her mouth. Her voice was strained and slightly hoarse when she tried to speak.

"Clive ... it's... a trap..." she gasped.

The mobster chuckled wickedly. My eyes were drawn to the terrace as a group of armed thugs emerged from the second level and hurried to the railing with their rifles pointed at us.

I stepped in front of Harriet and widened my body as much as possible in an attempt to shield her from their line of fire–though I doubted it would make much difference once the bullets started flying.

"I'm afraid this is the end of the line for you and Miss Doyel, detective," Malone said, picking the briefcase up off the ground, "Thank you for bringing me Lawrence's briefcase. Do me a favor. If either of you happen to see Mr. Daugherty when you arrive–wherever you end up–send him my best."

As he turned away, I called after him.

"Just tell me one thing, Malone. Was it you, or Daugherty who gave the order to have Midnight Lawrence murdered on New Year's Eve?"

Malone faced us once more.

"Daugherty wanted Lawrence dead, sure, but neither of us gave the official order to ice him. Actually, Riggs was the one who did the deed," he chuckled, "The funny thing about that is, he didn't realize he was the one Daugherty wanted dead, until after he'd killed him."

He glanced over at Riggs. "Do you want to tell them the real reason you strangled Lawrence that night, or should I?"

Riggs shifted uncomfortably, then finally said, "I thought he was trying to make a move on my girl. So I followed him into the washroom, strangled him with my belt, and then slipped out the window before anyone discovered the body. I took the whole day off—Never knew anyone was looking for him."

Malone laughed, "He's been working as a plant for Mr. Daugherty the whole time."

Something finally clicked in Harriet's head.

"So every time you were at my—Hal's Place, you were just snooping around for Daugherty?" she asked Riggs to confirm her suspicions.

"You were the one who helped the Black Clovers burn down Hal's Place," I realized.

Riggs grimaced, "I made sure Harriet wasn't there before I called the Clovers. Believe it or not, I do enjoy her performances..." He turned to Harriet, "I never wanted you to get involved in all this, dollface. I'm crazy about you! Besides, you deserve to be working for someone better than a man like Hal!"

Tears of fury filled the brunette's eyes. "I'm not your girl, Lenny! After everything you've done, I would never be with you! And, I never worked for Hal! I *am*—"

Malone held his hand and interrupted her before she could finish, "As entertaining as this little chat is, I have things to do and places to be."

He drew the brass key he'd taken from Harriet and placed it in one of the locks on the briefcase. To his surprise, the small key didn't unlock the lock. He fumbled around and tried the other lock. No luck!

"Come on! Open, damn it!" he shouted, as his frustration grew with each failed attempt. After several more attempts to pry the briefcase open, something finally registered. His eyes narrowed, and he scowled sourly at me, "This isn't Lawrence's briefcase! It's a fake! We've been had!"

He threw the briefcase aside, drew his pistol, and pointed it at me!

"Where is it?" he demanded, "What did you do with the real one?"

"You didn't really think I'd hand over evidence just like that, did you?" I said, "Terribly bad for business."

"I don't have time for this!" Malone yelled.

"No. You don't," I agreed.

"Ice them!"

Behind me, I heard Foster yell: "Chicago Police! Drop your weapons!"

Gunfire erupted from the terrace as the Black Clovers fired at the approaching uniformed officers.

In a second's time, a series of things happened at once:

Riggs sprinted toward Harriet.

Malone squeezed the trigger of his pistol.

Harriet screamed.

A bullet struck me in the chest.

Then, everything went black...

CHAPTER 21

The Hostile Hostage

"Hill! Hill!" John's voice echoed. He was kneeling beside me. "Officer down!"

My eyes fluttered open. I sat up with a groan, "I'm all right. Just got the wind knocked out of me."

John couldn't believe his eyes. "I saw you take a slug in the chest! How the Hell are you still alive?"

I reached into my coat and drew my cigarette case from the inner breast pocket of my jacket. The metal of the small silver case was dented with a bullet embedded in it. The skin underneath the layers of clothing was sore but remained otherwise uninjured—What difference would one more bruise make compared to all the other ones on my chest?

John chuckled and helped me to my feet, "You're one lucky son of a bitch!"

"How long was I out?" I asked.

"Only a few minutes."

"Did we get Malone?"

John nodded, "Yeah. We slapped a shiny pair of bracelets on him and took him and a couple of his pals into custody."

Looking around, I noticed Harriet was nowhere to be seen. "Where's Harriet?"

Foster frowned, "One of Malone's goons grabbed her and ran off on foot while we had our hands full with the button men on the terrace. He rabbited before we could get him."

"Then they can't have gotten far," I told him. Without any hesitation, I sprinted down the tunnel after Harriet and Riggs.

"Wait! Where are you going? Hill! Hill!" John called, but I was already halfway through the tunnel. I could hear him following closely behind me.

As we passed the other side, I immediately spotted Riggs struggling to get the brunette into a parked black vehicle nearby. Harriet was doing everything humanly possible to prevent herself from entering the car. Though her wrists were still bound, she was putting up one Hell of a fight.

The bony man grabbed the back of her skull and forcibly pushed her head through the open car door. Harriet responded accordingly by stretching her right foot behind her and thrusting it into Lenny's stomach. As he doubled over, the young woman tried to make a break for it. Before she took five steps away from him, Riggs seized a handful of Harriet's dress and yanked her back toward him.

"Let me go, Lenny!" she protested, kicking and thrashing her body violently.

"No!" Riggs barked, "You're coming with me! Now, get in the car!"

I thought that was as good a time as any to intervene. John and I crept forward with our revolvers drawn.

"It's over, Riggs!" I said in a loud voice, "You're surrounded! Let the girl go!"

Riggs spun Harriet around with his pistol drawn and pointed directly at her head. He ducked behind her, using her as a human shield—*the coward.*

Harriet looked at me with an expression that was a mix of fear, desperation, and relief at seeing me alive. Before that moment, she'd probably assumed I was dead. There were tears in her eyes.

"Clive?"

As much as I wanted to assure her that I had the situation under control, the gun pressed against her temple begged to differ.

"Not another step, coppers!" Riggs ordered, "You're not gonna take her from me! She's mine!"

"I'm not your girl!" the brunette yelled.

The bony man was clearly not in a sound state of mind. While it was clear that Harriet wanted out of the hostile situation, reminding her captor that she despised him and had no romantic feelings toward him would not get us anywhere. It was only going to escalate things more.

"Harriet, I need you to keep quiet for the next few minutes and let us do the talking," I said in a calm, level tone; my eyes never wavered from Riggs as I spoke, "Mr. Riggs is going through a lot right now. We don't want to say anything that'll upset him more..."

To my surprise, Harriet remained silent. I kept my focus on the man holding the gun to her head.

"Mr. Riggs—do you mind if I call you Lenny? —There's no need for violence..." I continued, treading carefully, "Let's talk like civilized human beings. You don't need to worry about Malone or anyone else butting in on our conversation. It's just us.

"I know you don't really want to hurt Miss Doyel. You're her biggest admirer, after all. Even when you were helping the Black Clovers, you made it a point to make sure that she wasn't anywhere near Hal's Place when they burned it down. You were trying to keep her safe."

The cogs were turning in Lenny's head. It looked like he was debating whether or not to take the gun off Harriet and point it at me—though that meant forfeiting the only leverage he had to do so. Riggs was not dimwitted enough to give that up. He kept the pistol pointed at the object of his affection.

"I know what a talented singer Miss Doyel is," I continued, "The first time you hear that voice of hers while she's in the limelight is sure to make any red-blooded man fall head-over-heels for her. It has a way of sticking in your head, like a pleasant thought that numbs everything else going through your mind. A woman like that has more power than any gangster in this city. She'd have the world at her feet.

"I understand how easy it is to become infatuated with someone like that. But, there are other dames in this city to choose from. What is it about Miss Doyel that has you coming back for more?"

Riggs was slightly perplexed by the question. "'You kidding me? Look at her. She's a dish! The moment I set my eyes on her; I knew she was the only dame I wanted."

It was true; she was a dish—and Lenny looked like he wanted to lick the plate and the rest of the dinner set that came with her until he'd satisfied his hunger. The man was as shallow as an undug well. The basis of his fixation on the young lounge singer seemed primarily physical. If I could keep him talking and focused on other things, hopefully, he'd let her go on his own and give himself up quietly once he started thinking clearly.

"I agree. Miss Doyel is quite the looker," I nodded, "I'm told you've attended most of her performances. It sounds like the two of you have known each other for quite a while."

The skinny man shook his head, "Nah. Only a few weeks. The first time I saw her was the night her boss opened Hal's Place."

"Sounds like there's a story there," I said, sounding interested, "I'd love to hear it."

Riggs had taken the bait. "I was there lookin' for any dirt that the Clovers could use as leverage to force Hal into reconsiderin' Mr. Daugherty's offer. While I was snoopin' around the club that night, I happened upon a lounge and was immediately drawn to the canary onstage. She was the kinda dame that men like me could only dream up on those cold, lonely nights..."

I wanted to vomit at whatever lude imagery he was insinuating but forced myself to continue listening.

"...After hearin' her sing, my ticker was beatin' a mile a minute. The look in her eyes told me she was enjoyin' the attention she was gettin'. Never seen a pretty dame look at me that way before."

"I see..."

"That night, I swore I was gonna make her my girl one way or another. No one was gonna come between me and her."

I raised my eyebrow. "I imagine that made things a bit more complicated with the Black Clovers..."

Riggs shrugged, "Got to see her a lot, so I'm not complaining."

"Is that why you were at the Bleeding Rose on New Year's Eve?" I asked, "Did Daugherty tell you to go there?"

He shook his head, "No. Like I said before, I took the whole day off. I just went because I'd heard she'd be singing there that night and didn't want to miss it."

"So you weren't aware that Daugherty sent Shifty-Shane and one of the other Clovers to kidnap Miss Doyel that night?"

This was news to him. That knowledge was apparently above his pay grade.

"No ... H-He wouldn't have ... He knew she was my girl."

I subtly shifted gears to keep him from getting too fixated on Harriet. "Lenny, why don't you tell me more about what happened with Lawrence that night."

"I never met the guy before, but I'd seen him once or twice at Hal's Place. I had no idea Mr. Daugherty was lookin' for him. I just thought he was some drunk trying to make a move on my girl. So I waited until he was alone and followed him into the washroom. The moment I saw him, I unfastened my belt and strangled him with it, until I knew he was dead. Then, slipped out of the window, got into a cab, and split."

"What about the fire?" I added, "I'm sure hearing Daugherty was planning on kidnapping Miss Doyel to find Lawrence's briefcase must've made you second-guess what you were doing?"

"I wasn't too keen on her getting dragged into all this, but the Clovers promised they were just gonna scare her into talkin'. She wasn't actually gonna get hurt."

Harriet scoffed.

"I volunteered to watch her apartment for the Clovers after Hal's Place went up in smoke," he continued, "I followed her cab when she headed over to the Palmer House last week and went inside. I tipped Malone off when I saw her head into the Empire Room. 'Hadn't expected to bump into you that night." He gave me the stink eye. "After I saw her leaving with another copper, I telephoned Mr. Daugherty and he sent Shifty-Shane over to her apartment. Once Mr. Daugherty got the briefcase, they were gonna let her go."

"And you'd be a shoulder for her to cry on..." I added.

"Exactly!" Riggs said excitedly. "But right after Shifty botched the kidnapping, she disappeared. I watched her apartment for days but didn't see her come or go."

I could tell Riggs was beginning to calm down a bit more. His grip on the pistol loosened as he continued.

"It wasn't until after Mr. Daugherty slept the big sleep that, someone finally spotted Miss Doyel leaving Police Headquarters with you and followed you both to the zoo. 'Got a call from Malone. He told me where you were. I hopped in my car and sped over there, lickety-split." He glanced at Harriet. "Malone knew you'd get spooked if anyone else approached you in broad daylight."

"I'm sure you were paid handsomely for it!" Harriet spat in disgust.

The skinny man looked at her, confused and slightly offended by the statement.

"You think this was about money?" Riggs said, "Sure, it might've started off that way, but not anymore. I meant what I said—I'm crazy about you, dollface. All this was to make sure you were safe. I'd never let anyone hurt you. Honest. You're the only dame I've ever wanted..."

Harriet rolled her eyes. After hearing the truth, every ounce of slight affection, pity, and tolerance she had for her overzealous admirer had been purged from her. Now, she was utterly disgusted by the man holding her at gunpoint. I could see that she wanted to say something in response. The anger and impatience on her face were growing by the minute.

Keep it together, I mentally pleaded with her; *just keep your trap shut. He's almost calm.*

"Don't you see..." the oblivious man continued, "now that Mr. Daughterty and Malone are out of the picture, you can finally be my girl. I'll make sure no one like them ever bothers you again."

That was the straw that broke the camel's back.

"I'm not your girl!" Harriet yelled, unable to keep silent any longer. "I never was!"

The confusion on Lenny's face only grew as the brunette laid it into him.

"Do you honestly think I would ever love you after everything you've put me through? You stupid bastard! You helped Daugherty burn down my club, killed my friends and my customers, and then helped the Black Clovers try to kidnap me twice!

"You sicken me! I'll never forgive you for what you've done! I hate you! There's a better chance of a snowball in Hell, than us ever being together! I will never be your girl!"

"Shit..." I thought out loud.

Riggs glowered at her. "What did you say?"

"I will never be your girl!" Harriet repeated, "I hate you!"

The bony man's knuckles tightened around the frame of the pistol. A cold, stoic rage covered his face. Tears of anger and pain filled his eyes, but he refused to let them fall. His jaw clenched.

"You ... You don't mean that... W-We're made for each other..."

Her defiant silence gave him the answer. It was not the one he wanted to hear. He took half a step to the right and held the pistol to the woman's temple.

"If I can't have you..." he said coldly, "... then no one can."

BANG!

The gunshot echoed in the cold night air and traveled over the waters of Lake Michigan until it finally dissipated. A body fell. To my surprise, it wasn't Harriet's, but Lenny Riggs's.

I glanced over my shoulder and saw the smoking barrel of John Foster's revolver, still pointed at where Riggs had been standing a moment earlier. The lifeless stiff of Lenny Riggs lay motionless on the cold pavement. His gaunt and narrow face was splattered with blood. The bullet that dropped him left a large, gory entry wound in one of his hollow eye sockets. A scarlet puddle began to form under his head.

"Nice shot," I admitted.

Foster slowly holstered his revolver and stared at the body.

"Thanks..." he said grimly, finding no pride in the sad circumstance he'd been forced to take.

After holstering my revolver, I hurried over to Harriet, who stood frozen. Apart from a few droplets of blood on her cheek, she, herself, had not been harmed. However, that didn't change the fact that I was still furious with her.

"What the Hell was that?" I shouted, "I told you to keep your mouth shut and let us handle it! But you just had to give Riggs your two cents, just as he was starting to calm down! You could've gotten yourself killed! How could you have been so stupid?"

I threw my arms around her and pulled her into a hug. Her reckless outburst had only escalated an already delicate situation and gotten someone killed. Thankfully, the only casualty had been the tragic soul holding her hostage. Had she not intervened, he, too, could have been saved. I sighed. At least Harriet was safe.

"I'm sorry. I'm sorry," she whimpered through teary eyes.

My anger quickly subsided. I could only guess what she had been through while in Malone's custody. As upset as I was that she'd gone off book with Riggs, she had every right to lash out at him the way she had. The man had a hand in sending her life off the rails.

"It's fine," I said calmly, "You're safe now. That's all that matters."

While I held her tightly, I stared down at her kidnapper's body. I couldn't help but feel a tiny sliver of pity for him. Lenny Riggs had been fueled by the natural desire to have what so many of us long for in this dark, dreary world: the need for love and companionship. He'd been deprived of both for so long that he became obsessed with the first poor dame who winked at him. He wanted it bad enough to kill for it if he believed someone was moving in his territory.

In an unfortunate misunderstanding, Riggs had followed Midnight Lawrence—a stranger, for the most part—into the washroom at the Bleeding Rose and strangled him to death with his belt, just for looking at Harriet. Little did he know that his crime of passion would uncover a much larger plot at play.

Although Lenny Riggs had not been a full-fledged member of the Black Clovers, he'd done atrocious acts for them, severe enough to earn him an equally guilty place in Hell. Besides being Lawrence's murder, Riggs had indirectly helped the Clovers burn down Harriet's club. That made him an accessory to murder, at the very least. In addition to the murder charges, he was also guilty of kidnapping her and threatening a police officer.

The funny thing was that we hadn't found any criminal record on him when we checked our files at the station. The man had been clean, so there was no reason to think otherwise. I had not suspected Riggs, and neither had Harriet. We had dismissed him as a harmless, overenthusiastic fan of her work with too much time on his hands. How wrong we'd been. He'd deceived us all, and people had died for it.

Now, he was lying in a puddle of his own blood.

After hearing the gunshot, a group of officers hurried to our location. Upon seeing the body, John brought them up to speed about what had occurred. Pictures of the body were taken for later review.

All the while, I walked Harriet away from the scene and kept her within arm's reach for the remainder of the night. With all that had happened recently, I was not letting her out of my sight again for a second.

CHAPTER 22

Frost on a Winter Rose

In the weeks that followed, things began to settle down. All the evidence I'd collected during the case and Malcolm Malone's public confession were enough to incriminate the Black Clovers, their late boss, and himself. Because of this, Malone and the remaining Black Clovers were tried for their crimes, convicted on multiple counts, and given matching striped pajamas to wear while they did heavy time behind bars. Despite his attempts to bribe and finagle his way out of his sentence, the charges stuck to Malone like burs on a tweed suit. I took great satisfaction in knowing that someone would be serving Cyrus Daugherty's lifetime sentence for him. Justice had been done.

Once everything was smoothed out, Captain Shoemaker arranged for Harriet to stay at another apartment in the city until the repairs to her place were finished. From what I'd seen, her new living space was far less roomy than her old one. Fortunately for her, it was only temporary.

Harriet and I saw a lot of each other after the trial. For the most part, Harriet had given up any ambitions of resuming her secret life as a club owner and, instead, decided to focus on her promising career as a lounge singer—though that didn't stop her from complaining about having to tighten her belt whenever her landlord came by to collect rent. Whenever neither of us was busy working, we spent as much free time together as possible. Many of my colleagues were not shy about showing their surprise when they learned I was seeing Harriet exclusively—but that was to be expected.

Since closing the Lawrence Case, we shared more than a couple of tender embraces and a handful of intimate moments. The romance was very much alive. For the first time, I found myself in a committed relationship. As enjoyable as it was, something in my mind continued to trouble me—though I did my best to ignore it.

That Valentine's Day, we decided to meet at the Chez Paree Nightclub for dinner. As luck would have it, one of Harriet's old school chums worked as a dancer in the "Adorables," which performed there every evening. Wanting to make the night memorable, Harriet telephoned her to see if she could get us a table for two. I figured it would be a long shot but didn't see any harm in trying—it was our first Valentine's Day together. After pulling a few strings, her friend was able to sweet-talk one of the owners, Mike Fritzel, into scaring up a table for us on such short notice. It seemed it was going to be a memorable evening indeed.

Valentine's Day was never one of my favorite holidays. Even before Capone had seven of Moran's men killed on the North Side in a bloody massacre five years ago, the holiday never had much appeal to me. All the romance and affection just seemed like another excuse for hard-working fellas to waste loads of cash on silly things like flowers and chocolates to satisfy the dame you're with for one night. You could just as easily spend a pleasant evening with a stranger without the constraints of being in a relationship during that time—no shrubs or sweets necessary.

Now, things were different. I was no longer a carefree bachelor. By some miracle, I had a Valentine to spend the holiday with. Everything about it was new to me. I wanted to ensure I did everything right for our special evening together.

I entered the restaurant's main room with a single winter rose. I'd spent half an hour or so waiting in line with every other mug in this city trying to pick up a few last-minute gifts for that special someone in their life. While many paid top dollars for embarrassingly overpriced carnations of flowers, I thought a single rose felt more appropriate for the occasion.

As you know, Chicago has many high-end restaurants that are the perfect spot for a romantic evening. Many of which are as enjoyable as a glass of fine wine. So, believe me when I tell you that the Chez Paree was a bottle of top-shelf champagne by comparison. The supper club was located on the third floor of the Fairbanks Court building, where its glamorous atmosphere became legendary. It certainly earned its reputation as "Chicago's Smartest Supper Club."

Large curtains served as the backdrop for the stage, with a larger extension behind them that created more room for extensive performances. Smaller curtains covered the stage's wings, allowing the dancers and performers to go to and fro during each act. A pair of curved stairs framed the ground-level orchestra pit and rose from the hardwood dance floor to the top of the stage.

The main room alone could accommodate 650 people, not including the waitstaff. Clean tablecloths covered the surrounding tables and gave all its patrons a clear view of the stage, no matter where they were seated. I was very impressed by the systematic movements of the servers as they carried trays and drinks to each of the tables—not once bumping into each other in the crowded restaurant. Watching them work was almost as entertaining as the floor show.

I approached the counter at the front of the restaurant, where a sharply dressed host stood. He looked up at me and smiled.

"Good evening, sir. Do you have a reservation?"

"I should. I'm meeting someone here tonight."

"Splendid! What name is the reservation under?"

"Doyel. It should be a table for two."

The man nodded.

"Ah, yes. Right this way. Miss Doyel is waiting for you."

The host led me to a private table near the edge of the dancefloor, where a brunette beauty awaited me.

Harriet was dressed in a nice little blue number. Her blue silk dress was covered in floret-shaped sequins. The straps on her shoulders were covered in blue rhinestones, which shimmered in the light. The dress itself hugged the curves of her body, particularly around the chest and waist area, and fanned out at the knee like a cascade of falling water. Her dark hair fell to the sides of her head in romantic waves and stopped at the nape of her neck. A touch of navy-blue eyeshadow had been applied above her eyes in a way that made the dark brown of her irises pop in contrast with her light skin. Light rouge emphasized her sharp cheekbones. Luscious lips decorated in raspberry-red lipstick parted into a vibrant smile as soon as she saw me.

"Darling! You made it!" she beamed and threw her arms around me.

"Sorry, I'm late," I apologized, "Traffic was murder." I handed the rose to her. "Here. I picked this up for you on my way over."

"It's beautiful!" she said, happily kissing my lips, "I love it! Thank you!"

I breathed a sigh of relief. "Glad you like it."

"Now that you're here, would you care to join me?"

Nodding, I hurried to the other side of the table and pulled out Harriet's chair for her. Once she was seated, I occupied the chair across from her.

"What did I miss?" I asked, glancing at the stage.

"Only, one of the most elaborate dance numbers I've seen!" she exclaimed, "Gosh—The costumes! The choreography! I can't even begin to describe it to you! It was the cat's pajamas!"

"Pity I missed it," I said, "Sounds like they pulled out all the stops."

Truthfully, I never cared much for big, showy dance numbers, so I wasn't too torn up about missing their performance. Still, there was no denying that the Chez Paree Adorables were some of the most talented dancers in this city. At the very least, Harriet was able to watch her friend perform while I was away. There would surely be plenty of other entertainment for us to enjoy that evening.

My thoughts were interrupted when our waiter appeared a moment later.

"Good evening and welcome to the Chez Paree. I'll be your server this evening. Can I get either of you something to drink tonight?"

"The lady will have a dry martini," I said, recalling her favorite drink.

Harriet smiled coyly and added, "And he'll have an old-fashioned. Be a dear and make sure to use your best whiskey."

The young server nodded, "Of course. I'll be back with your drinks in a moment."

For the next few minutes, the stunning woman across from me stared at me silently with a satisfied grin.

"What is it? Do I have something on my face?" I asked while attempting to use my napkin to wipe away any lipstick stuck to my lips.

The beautiful brunette just giggled, "No. I was just admiring how handsome you look tonight. I've never seen this side of you, Clive Hill. Very dapper."

I humbly brushed off her compliment and took it with a grain of salt. Like all the other male patrons in the restaurant, I was dressed in a black dinner jacket, matching trousers, a vest, and a white button-down wingtip shirt. Additionally, a black bowtie hung at my collar. I didn't normally enjoy getting so dressed up; I'd have been much more comfortable in one of my usual suits, but Harriet insisted that I look my best. She certainly did.

"You clean up pretty nice yourself," I said with a smile, "That dress is sensational. The way it dazzles, people might think you're here to sing."

Her eyes glittered with wonder at the thought. "That would be a dream! Can you imagine it ... Me, performing up there? I'd just die!"

Just then, a beautiful girl with a camera wandered over to our table.

"The two of you make such a lovely couple. Would you like a photograph so you can remember your night at the Chez?" she asked.

Harriet clapped her hands together in excitement. "Oh, yes, please!"

I scooched closer and placed my arm around her as the camera girl took the picture. Once our eyes recovered from the camera's flash, the girl handed us a small card with a number.

"I'll be back in twenty minutes with your memory," she said before continuing.

The waiter returned with our drinks not two minutes after she'd walked away.

"Here you are," he said, placing two glasses before us, "Can I get you anything else?"

I quickly read the menu and knew what I wanted to order.

"I'll have the Pepper Steak Special," I said, handing him the menu.

The waiter turned to Harriet. "And for you, madam?"

The exceptionally stunning brunette agonized over her decision for a moment more. Eventually, she settled on a choice.

"Hmmm ... I'm going to go with the smoked salmon and a house salad."

"Excellent," the man said, tucking her menu under his arm, "I'll have those put in for you both right away."

He turned and headed toward the kitchen without another word, leaving us alone again.

I lifted my glass to propose a toast.

"To the first of many holidays together," I said, "Happy Valentine's Day, doll."

Harriet raised her martini and touched her glass to mine with a slight *clink*.

"Happy Valentine's Day."

The moment my drink passed my lips, there was no denying that quality whiskey had been used. The smokey bitters created a pleasant aroma and flavor that balanced everything. The drink was subtly sweeter, with notes of vanilla, oak, caramel, and the faintest hint of apple. If I had to guess, I'd have said the bartender had used bourbon instead of the typical whiskey in most places around the city. All in all, it went down very smoothly.

"That's a damn good drink," I said to myself and took another sip.

Just then, the lights dimmed, and the orchestra played a drumroll. A bright spotlight directed everyone's attention to the stage. The new emcee, Jack Waldron, stood at the right side of the stage. He was dressed as nicely as everyone in the joint, with a clean dinner jacket and bowtie. Despite his sparkling smile, he seemed nervous about performing at Chicago's most innovative restaurant and supper club. From what I'd read in the papers, he and his wife, Harriet Waldron, were used to working in much smaller venues.

"Ladies and Gentlemen, we have a very special treat this evening! The Society Maestro and his crew invite all the couples here tonight to the dance floor for a Valentine's Day dance! Please put your hands together for the Society Maestro himself, Mister Vincent Lopez!"

As the curtain swung open, the famous maestro stood at his piano and bowed to the audience before he sat on the bench again. Vincent Lopez was dressed in a solid black dinner jacket with long tails that flowed behind him. He wore matching dress pants, with a white dress shirt, and bowtie the color of freshly fallen snow. His black hair had been slicked back tightly over his scalp. A bright rose, not unlike the one I'd given Harriet, was pinned to the collar of his jacket. He was dressed to the nines and then some.

The applause was thunderous! Considering that the Society Maestro and his crew would be leaving the Chez Paree next week to return to the St. Regis in New York, seeing them perform tonight would undoubtedly be a treat. For many, it would be their last chance to watch Lopez and his crew perform. Harriet could barely contain her excitement.

Taking Harriet's soft hand in mine, I led her away from our table and onto the dance floor as the crowd gathered. Even Jack Waldron and his wife took to the dance floor. No one wanted to miss out on the fun. Harriet turned and faced me, then took a step closer. My other hand moved to the small of her back. Her warm skin was as smooth as the blue silk fabric of her dress.

The orchestra began to play *Lonesome Lover* for the gathering couples. As soon as the music started, our bodies moved in step. Harriet and I swayed to the rhythm as naturally as the tide against the shore. Rocking back and forth, our movements mirrored each other with grace.

A laugh escaped Harriet's mouth as I swung us around suddenly in a half-turn, then spun in the opposite direction. She had not expected the spin but managed to keep her balance. Her face was beaming with euphoric delight, so much so, that she threw her head back as we spun again.

I was enjoying myself as well. Our feet moved like they'd been enchanted. Moreover, something about losing ourselves to the music was almost magic. We were so focused on the swell time we were having that I couldn't tell you who was singing the vocals that Jack Parker had made famous when the song was first recorded.

Before we knew it, the song came to an end.

After the dance, everyone returned to their seats. Lopez and his crew started their next song, but I was too focused on other things to have been able to tell you its name. Our attention was drawn to the waiter as he brought our dinner over. He vanished as quickly as he appeared once our food was on the table.

Harriet took in all the sights of the Chez Paree: The lights. The music. The architecture. Her mouth widened in amazement.

"Isn't this place just lovely?" She didn't wait for my reply. "If I ever rebuild Hal's Place, I want it to look more like this."

The statement had caught me a little off-guard. Harriet hadn't talked about rebuilding Hal's Place in weeks. She'd been so quiet about it that I'd thought she'd let it go and move on to other endeavors. However, it seemed that was not the case.

"Sounds expensive," I said, trying not to give the topic too much attention. That didn't stop Harriet.

"So tell me, darling, whatever happened to Midnight Lawrence's briefcase?" she asked, "Now that the case is over, there can't be much use for that old thing."

I sighed. I'd hoped to avoid talking about it with her now that things were cooling down. There was only one direction this conversation was headed in, and despite my attempt to subvert it, I was just along for the ride.

"It's been put into storage. Commissioner Allman made sure that all of Daugherty's ledgers were analyzed further and ended up in safe hands."

"What about Daugherty's fortune?" she pried, "Where did all that money end up?"

I shook my head disapprovingly and took another swig of my drink before answering.

"The City has divided all of it up and put it toward a number of charitable organizations. Outside of that, I couldn't tell you."

"I still don't think that's fair," Harriet pouted, "A portion of that money should've been given to me. I think I'm owed that much. I could've used it to—"

"I didn't come here to talk shop," I said plainly, making no attempt to hide my annoyance, "I thought we were here to celebrate Valentine's Day together."

The lingering thoughts in the back of my mind slowly began to resurface.

Harriet sighed, "You're right. I'm sorry. I shouldn't have brought it up."

"I thought you were going to focus on your singing career," I reminded her.

"I am..."

She paused momentarily, as if fighting the urge to say more.

"It's just ... I'm used to having so much more money than I'm making now. It would just be nice to get all that I'm owed."

Before I could say anything more, the camera girl returned to our table with a photograph.

"Here you are," the woman said, handing the developed photograph to Harriet, "Sorry about the wait. There was a mix-up with a couple of the other memories. But here is yours."

The "memory" was much more expensive than you would've expected—far more than I care to share. I sighed and handed the girl a couple of bills.

"Thank you," she said, placing the money in one of her pockets, "Enjoy the rest of your evening. Happy Valentine's Day."

With that, she walked away.

Harriet sat and admired the photograph for a moment.

"Look at us. We do make a handsome couple. Don't you think?" she sighed, "This'll be a fine memory indeed. It ought to be framed. Would you like to see it?"

I shook my head. The price I paid for it was memory enough for me.

The stunning brunette stood up. "If you'll excuse me, I need to find the ladies' room."

"I'll be here," I assured her.

A few minutes after Harriet stepped away, a beautiful blonde cigarette girl made her rounds by my table.

"Cigars? Cigarettes?" she called.

She was dressed in a low décolletage and short draped skirt. To say the woman had been *blessed* in certain *areas* of her life would have been an understatement. The girl had the curves of a smooth ceramic vase. She put Harriet to shame. A long strap rounded the back of her neck and connected to a tray carrying trinkets, cigars, cigarettes, and other memorabilia. She noticed that I was alone.

"Hello there, handsome," she said with a twinkle in her eye. "What are you doing all alone tonight?"

Her voice had a husky tone to it that was pleasing to the ears. Combined with the rest of her womanly features, she was easy on the eyes. She was the kind of girl the old Clive Hill would've taken home in a heartbeat. Unfortunately for her, I was already with someone tonight.

"Just waiting for my date," I told her, "She should be back in a few minutes."

The blonde woman frowned slightly at the news but focused on the business.

"Can I get you any cigars or cigarettes? Maybe a couple of trinkets to remember tonight while you're waiting?"

A small blue matchbook caught my eye as I perused the items in her tray. Upon closer inspection, I noticed the words *Chez Paree Chicago* printed in gold letters on the top flap of it. It couldn't have been as expensive as the photograph I'd purchased. Harriet had her trinket; it only seemed fair that I picked up something for myself.

"Just the matches," I said, handing her some change.

The blonde placed the change on her tray. She glanced at me once more and struck a subtle yet seductive pose for me.

"Are you sure there's nothing else here that catches your eye?" she said coyly.

Boy was there, but I willed myself to look away from her before I started thinking with something other than my head.

"I'm afraid not," I said politely, "Enjoy your night."

Before pocketing the matchbook, I flipped it between my fingers several times, admiring it from all sides. It was a meager souvenir but a practical one that I would enjoy.

Out of the corner of my eye, I noticed Harriet return to the table. From the look of things, she had done more than touch up her makeup during her absence. The scent of new rose perfume wafted through the air.

"You look refreshed," I told her, noting the satisfied smile on her face.

"I am," she agreed, "I met the sweetest attendant in the ladies' room. She was such a big help. I feel as pampered as a princess!"

It looked like it. If you'd sprinkled a dash of pixie dust on her, she likely would've started floating in the air at that very moment.

"New perfume?" I asked.

"Yes. Do you like it? The attendant had a brand-new bottle and I had to buy it!" Her train of thought wandered for a brief second. "I'll have to remember to hire one like that when I rebuild—" She stopped herself before she finished. "Sorry."

"Harriet," I said after a short moment of silence, "What do you say we get out of here?"

The question caught the brunette off-guard. She quickly glanced over at the stage.

"What about the rest of the show?"

"There will be others."

Harriet studied my face with a look of concern. "Are you feeling all right?"

"I'm fine," I assured her, "Just need some air is all."

After settling the bill, we gathered our belongings and retrieved our coats from the coatroom. We took the elevator to the lobby and exited together. We spent the entire trip downstairs in silence.

The night air was brisk and not at all unpleasant as we walked outside. Harriet and I continued down the block until we came to a quiet little corner under a streetlight. It was well-lit with no one else around.

Harriet's blue dress sparkled in the light like tiny stars dancing around her. She looked wonderful.

"Mind telling me why you brought me out here?" she asked.

"I just wanted to talk," I said.

She eyed me suspiciously. "Is it a conversation we could've had in the nice warm nightclub, instead of the cold?"

I shrugged, "Too many distractions in there. Besides, I wanted you to be able to hear me."

A thousand things were running through my head at that moment. All of them were about Harriet.

The hesitant look on her face remained as she dared to venture further into the conversation.

"All right. What do you want to talk about?"

I did my best to collect my jumbled thoughts. My pulse quickened. My gloved hands suddenly went clammy.

"There's ... something I've been meaning to ask you..." I started, "Something that's been on my mind ever since we took down Malone and the Black Clovers."

The words fumbled around on the tip of my tongue. It was hard to decide which ones to use and which were better off being omitted entirely. What I wanted to ask was far too important to risk getting wrong. I nervously toyed with the contents of my pocket while I sorted through my head.

All the while, Harriet stared at me, attempting to read my thoughts. Her eyes suddenly widened, and a smile crept across her face as she arrived at a conclusion.

"Oh my goodness!" The excitement in her voice grew. "Are you going to ask what I think you're going to ask?"

She was practically jumping up and down.

"I—I can't believe this is really happening!" Harriet exclaimed with tears of joy in her eyes.

The excited woman moved in to kiss me, but before she could, I mustered the courage to ask my question.

"Why'd you do it?

The question caught Harriet entirely by surprise. The smile on her face vanished while the look of confusion returned. Whatever she'd been expecting to hear had fallen short in reality.

"W—What?" she stammered.

"Why did you do it?" I asked again.

"Clive, I—I don't understand..."

"The morning we went to the zoo, you and I were alone in my office..."

Memory slowly began to return to her as I continued.

"...When you found Lawrence's briefcase, you asked me a series of questions—not unlike the ones you asked me tonight. While we were at the zoo later that morning, you slipped your hand into my pocket and took the key to it while we kissed." I bit my lip before continuing, "Did you think that I wouldn't find out?"

Her face paled. "I-I..."

I shook my head disapprovingly. "After everything we've been through ... Why did you do it? Why'd you steal the key?"

There was deep regret in the young woman's eyes. She stood in silence, either trying to deny her crime or formulating all the facts before she gave her argument. I wasn't entirely sure if her silence was meant to spite me or buy time for herself. Whatever the reason, she knew there was no way of escaping it.

Frustration and heartbreak cut me to the core. I couldn't even bring myself to look at her anymore.

"I want the truth," I told her.

Harriet sighed in defeat, "I needed those ledgers. Each of those books contained enough information to access all of Daugherty's bank accounts. With just one of them, I'd have enough money to rebuild my club. If Lawrence had sold them to me, just like we planned, I'd be sitting pretty."

She looked at me with pleading eyes. What were once tears of joy quickly became tears of remorse.

"I'd lost so much ... I—I didn't know where else to get the money. I wasn't thinking clearly."

My eyes met hers once more. "You used me."

"No!"

"You manipulated me and stole from me. Did that kiss mean anything, or was it just so you could get close enough to pick my pocket?"

"How could you even think that?" she gasped, unable to mask the pain in her voice, "There's more to me than just money. I haven't always thought about rebuilding my club."

"You could've fooled me. That's all you've been talking about tonight," I pointed out, "You just couldn't help yourself. Were we really going to celebrate the holiday together, or was all this so you could corner me and keep asking questions all night?"

"What are you talking about?"

"You know exactly what I'm talking about," I pushed, "You seemed more concerned about making plans for your club tonight than you have been about us. I'm not playing second fiddle to a stack of brick-and-mortar."

The thoughts in my head flowed more freely. A renewed clarity focused them as I searched for answers.

"Has everything about our relationship been one big elaborate con to get your hands on Lawrence's briefcase?" I asked, feeling a twinge of pain, "Was the romance a lie too?"

The tears in Harriet's eyes ran down her face like water from a leaky faucet.

"Of course not! It's real!" she cried, "It always has been! Do you think so little of me?"

I shook my head and tried to make sense of everything. "Honestly ... I don't know what to think. You rack up enough lies, it starts to get difficult to tell when you're telling the truth."

My thoughts continued to wander as I confronted all the questions plaguing my mind.

"Maybe it's my fault..." I told myself out loud, "I let my guard down and let myself believe there was someone out there who wanted the same thing I did."

"I do!"

A sad sigh escaped my lungs, "If that were true, you wouldn't have taken the key from me. The thing that stings the most, is you thought you'd get away with it without me knowing. What kind of a relationship is that?"

"Clive, please," Harriet pleaded, "Please don't do this ..."

Her attempts to sway me were brushed aside. I stood there feeling as cold and solid as a block of ice. My breath was troubled, while my pulse quickened. It was as if I'd forgotten how to breathe entirely. The chill filling me was so cold that it was almost painful.

"I tried to ignore it. Tried to make things work. But I haven't been able to look past what you did. The line you crossed ... there's no coming back from that ... and you'll have to live with the consequences."

Fear flickered in Harriet's brown eyes. "Are—Are you going to arrest me?"

"I could. You did steal evidence," I reminded her, "But after everything we've been through ... I can't."

A lump of sadness grew in my throat. It threatened to keep the words I dreaded from leaving my lips. The will it took to force them out of my mouth was more than any physical feat I'd ever had to overcome. I'd given more of my heart to Harriet than any other woman. The fact that I found myself in this unfortunate situation was tearing me apart. In my sadness, I looked away from her once again. Seeing her face was far too painful.

"But none of it changes the fact that you betrayed me," I finally said, "You let your selfishness drive a wedge between us. I can't stand here and pretend that what you did doesn't bother me. You burned me. Plain and simple.

"I thought I knew who you were, but now ... I'm not so sure. How can I stay with a woman who caresses my cheek with one hand, and uses the other to stab me in the back a moment later?"

Despite everything telling me not to, I forced myself to look at Harriet.

"I want to believe that everything that happened between us was real ... but, sadly ... I can't trust you."

Of all the days to break a dame's heart, doing it on Valentine's Day was especially cold, even by my standards. Unfortunately, I had to be a cold-hearted bastard to do it, but it needed to be done. In the end, there was no avoiding it.

I watched as the frost of grief consumed the winter rose, I had considered my love. Its icy blanket slowly drained the vibrant life from her as she processed what had just happened.

For a moment, we stood in silence. We were still trying to figure out what to say next.

"I'm ... sorry that it has to be this way," I said, breaking the quiet lull. There wasn't much more to say.

As much as I cared about Harriet, the sad truth was that there was no future with someone I couldn't trust—not that our relationship had started with a healthy foundation. When we first met, Harriet had already woven an intricate web of deception around herself. She'd been concealing her identity from everyone in the city by using a proxy to stand in for her while running her business. That, in itself, should've been a clear indicator that she was untrustworthy.

Looking back, it was hard to tell what was real between us and what had been a series of lies and manipulations she'd used to achieve her goals. Had any of it been real? Whatever the truth was, it didn't change anything.

"I should go," Harriet said, turning to leave.

"Can I call you a cab?" I offered.

She shook her head. "No. I drove here myself."

I'd half expected those to be the last words she ever said to me as I watched her walk away from me. On her fifth step, though, she paused and glanced over her shoulder.

"Clive, I meant everything I said ... I really do love you."

The heartbreak in her words hit like a stiff fist thrusted straight through my chest. It was far worse than the beating Malone's goons had given me a month ago.

"I know ... I did too," I said sadly, "Take care of yourself."

Harriet gave a brief nod, then continued on her way. The rose in her hand slipped through her fingers and fell onto the cold sidewalk. She did not attempt to retrieve it or slow her pace. She simply left it behind, forsaking all the memories associated with it.

Harriet and I were over. Instead of hailing a cab, as I'd done earlier, I walked home on foot. My steps were heavy, and the path was bitter, but I knew the way. It had been a difficult decision, though I knew I'd made the right one. 'Didn't mean it didn't hurt like Hell.

I never saw Harriet Doyel again. I'm told she packed everything a few days later and moved to the Big Apple for a fresh start. She never did end up rebuilding Hal's Place. That dream died the same night as our relationship. Wherever she ended up, I genuinely hope she found happiness. She at least deserved that much.

CHAPTER 23

Only Time Will Tell

The following morning, I clocked in at work. Although my love life had fallen to pieces, the world was still turning. Being alone at home and moping around wouldn't do me any good. The best thing I could do was to keep myself busy. At least at work, I could be productive.

Overall, things in the department were quiet, but not unusually so. The *clicking* and *clacking* of typewriter keys could still be heard throughout the bullpen while secretaries and other dicks typed up reports. A handful simply sat at their desks, sipped on steaming beverages, and chatted with the people around them. It was just a typical day at the office.

While all that was going on, I casually walked over to one of the nearby pots of coffee and poured myself a cup. It had been a rough night, even after ending things with Harriet. For most of it, I'd found myself lying awake in bed with my thoughts, going over every possible way I could've done things differently, but all of them eventually arrived at the same conclusion.

The little sleep I did get was hardly enough to rejuvenate my weary body, nor had it relieved my troubled mind. It was a miracle I'd even stumble into the Headquarters building that morning.

I pressed the cup of joe to my lips, slowly tilted it back, and let its contents slide down my throat. It was the only thing keeping me awake. The more of it I drank, the easier it was to pass as a functional member of society.

After pouring myself a second mug, I wandered to Foster's office and knocked on the door.

"Come in."

John was seated at his desk when I entered. His navy suit jacket was draped over the back of his chair, and his red suspenders could be seen while he worked diligently at his desk.

"Got a minute?" I asked.

The other detective looked up at me. "Of course.

I glanced over at the small stack of papers on his desk.

"Are you sure? I can always come by another time."

"Nonsense," he assured me, pushing the papers aside, "Just wrapping up a few minor reports. Nothing that needs to be done today."

I stepped further into the office, shut the door behind me, and then occupied the chair across from him.

John smiled warmly, "Say, how'd your date with Harriet go last night?"

My eyes looked away from him hesitantly.

"That bad, huh?" he deduced.

"Worse," I stated, "Things started off well—I gave her a rose, we did a little dancing—but during dinner, her focus was on other things."

"What do you mean?"

I sighed, "All she wanted to talk about was the Midnight Lawrence case. As it turns out, she's still thinking about rebuilding Hal's Place."

"You're kidding..."

"Nope," I said, shaking my head, "Instead of enjoying our evening together, the only thing on her mind was all the changes she wanted to make to the club when it's rebuilt. Despite several attempts to change the topic with her, we always arrived right back at the start. It was like being stuck on a merry-go-round, only far less enjoyable."

John nodded understandably. "I've been in a few conversations like that myself with Evalyn. They can be very exhausting."

"I confronted Harriet about stealing the keys..." I told John.

His eyes widened with interest. "You did? And ... How'd that go?"

"As well as you'd expect." I lit a cigarette and blew some smoke into the air. "It broke her heart. I'm sure she hates me for it."

"Don't say that," he said, easing my troubled mind, "You know how women get when they're upset. Why don't you give it a few days? Let her cool down. Then—"

"It's over, John," I said plainly, "I ended things with Harriet last night. I just ... couldn't trust her."

"Well ... You should've led with that." He studied my face for a moment. "Sorry to hear that, Clive. How are you holding up?"

I shrugged, "It comes and it goes. But it was the right call."

Another cloud of smoke passed my lips. "Never thought I'd make it this far with a woman. Guess I'm just meant to be a bachelor."

"The year's still young," John pointed out, "I'm sure the right dame is out there waiting for you. Harriet just wasn't it. Trust me, Clive, you'll find her eventually."

As much as I wanted to believe those words, the pain in my heart made that seem unlikely. Before Harriet, being in a genuine relationship was foreign to me. But, once I was in one, it wasn't all that bad. I enjoyed it.

Maybe John was right. Maybe the right dame is somewhere out there waiting for me. Maybe not. Only time will tell.

In the meantime, there was plenty to do to keep myself busy. Lord knows, crime in this city never sleeps. I still had work to do.

John let me mull my thoughts over without interruption. That was something I'd come to respect about him. He knew when to speak and when to stay silent.

After a moment, he leaned forward.

"You gonna be all right, Clive?"

"Yeah..." I sighed. "I'll be fine."

I stood up and started toward the door.

"Well," I said, glancing at my wristwatch, "I'll let you get back to your reports. I didn't mean to take up too much of your time."

"You didn't," he assured me, "I'm always willing to lend an ear."

As soon as I reached the door, he stopped me again.

"Hey. What'd you say tomorrow night we go out and grab a couple of drinks to take your mind off of things?" he said, trying to lighten the mood, "The first round's on me."

It was a kind gesture. One that I was honestly considering. After weighing the options, I decided it was best to keep myself social.

"All right," I said, "Tomorrow night, it is."

John smiled widely.

"All right, then. I was thinking we could try that new bar at the Drake, the Coq d'Or. How does that sound?"

For the first time in what felt like ages, I chuckled. "As long as you're buying."

"Hey, tomorrow's your day," he laughed, "Like I said, the first round's on me."

Even after leaving John's office, the smile on my face remained. Sure, I was still upset that Harriet and I didn't work out, but the old proverb says that when life gives you a stack of lemons, the best thing to do is make lemonade. There were bound to be bad days—that's life—however, it's the people you share those terrible days with that help you get through them.

I don't know what the future holds for me. Can any of us honestly say for sure? Maybe there'll be romance, maybe not. Whatever it has in store, one truth remains: tomorrow is a new day.